THE LIES SHE TOLD

A PSYCHOLOGICAL SUSPENSE THRILLER

N. L. HINKENS

Text copyright @ 2019 Norma Hinkens

Published by Dunecadia Publishing, California

ISBN: 978-1-947890-15-2

Cover by: **www.derangeddoctordesign.com**

Editing by: **www.jeanette-morris.com/first-impressions-writing**

❀ Created with Vellum

PROLOGUE

They dubbed themselves the quad squad back in their sophomore year of high school—Lachlan, Tina, Vivian and herself—priding themselves on their mean girl reputation. In retrospect, hit squad would have been a more apt name for them. They terrorized the campus in their own twisted way—their razor-sharp quips slashing their most vulnerable peers like blades, ostracizing the lonely to the point of despair, circulating the kind of lurid rumors that soured and spread more quickly than spilled milk. Those who crossed them or underestimated their sway became their next unwitting targets.

Haley had felt pressured into upping the ante that day—a day now seared in her memory for all the wrong reasons. She'd tried too hard to impress her quad sisters and it had backfired in the most horrific way possible. For the rest of their lives, they were forced to share a dark secret they'd sworn never to speak of again.

$\mathcal{H}$aley's fingers wouldn't stop shaking as she applied her amethyst eyeliner. She'd finally landed her dream job. Today was her first day working as a paralegal for the reputable law firm Huntington and Dodd. The field of law hadn't always interested her, but through her volunteer work with Big Brothers Big Sisters, she'd developed a heart to see justice served on behalf of those who deserved it. Ironic, considering the fact that she'd never paid the price for what she'd done eleven years ago in high school. Sure, she'd made every effort to atone for her actions in other ways, but guilt still dogged her like a ball and chain on the dark days when the memories came rushing back like an angry mob bent on her destruction.

Participating in Big Brothers Big Sisters gave her the opportunity to mentor kids and help them understand their value as human beings. If she'd had a little more self-esteem back in high school, maybe she wouldn't have felt the compulsion to impress her "quad sisters" in increasingly reckless ways. *Sisters* was a stretch. She'd never really felt close to any of them but being the target of their ridicule was too stomach-churning an alternative to contemplate. When Lachlan, Tina and Vivian had invited her into their inner circle, she'd worked hard to be accepted by them—learned to dress like them, talk like them, walk like them, enjoy what they enjoyed, hate who they hated. Somewhere in the process, she'd lost her soul. That's the only way she could account for what she'd done that awful day.

Haley reached for a makeup remover wipe and went about cleaning up the slovenly job she'd made of her left eye. Afterward, she studied her face in her magnifying mirror. Amethyst was a good color for green eyes, and the over-priced La Mer foundation that the sales assistant had assured her felt like a "second skin" had indeed furnished her with a silky, movie-star complexion that blended away her smattering of freckles. Her chestnut hair clustered around her shoulders in seemingly effortless waves that had taken a good twenty minutes to create. She needed to look the part, and that meant blending in without looking like she was trying too hard—an art she had perfected for better or worse.

She sighed as she tidied away her makeup brushes. Everything was coming together now that she'd landed the perfect job. But, at moments like this—when life was everything she'd hoped it would be—her heart was heaviest. Thanks to her, Emma Murray was never going to experience landing her dream job, or meeting the love of her life, or any of a hundred other things on Haley's extensive bucket list.

Beneath the surface, she felt undeserving of happiness when good things happened to her. She was a fraud. Some days she even felt like a monster. The shame persisted, even as the memories faded to the point where some days, Haley wondered if it had happened at all. Her therapist had encouraged her to use her remorse as a tool to re-examine her past behavior so she didn't end up making the same mistake twice, and then move on. But Haley had only told her she'd destroyed a friendship—the tip of the iceberg. She could never tell anyone the truth. And neither would her quad sisters. That was the one thing she could count on.

She slipped on her jacket and exited her house, locking the front door behind her. It still gave her a thrill each time she turned the key in the lock. She'd only moved in a couple of months earlier, purchasing the house with the help of a generous down payment from her parents, who'd retired from their high-powered jobs and relocated to Florida. They had since bought a townhouse on the intracoastal waterway and had thrown themselves into the boating lifestyle. Haley was also enjoying her newfound freedom—being the only child in her parents' spotlight had come with certain obligations when they lived in close proximity. It had taken all of her willpower not to tell them what she'd done to Emma Murray.

Her new home was located in a relatively quiet cul-de-sac. In the short time she'd lived here, she'd been too preoccupied with work and volunteering to get to know any of the neighbors well. The single man on her left worked a night shift and most likely slept most of the day. She'd deduced that the elderly couple on her right were either recluses or too sickly to socialize as they kept their curtains drawn day and night. The family across the street had waved at her as they all piled into their minivan headed to a soccer game one Saturday, and she'd briefly exchanged pleasantries with the young couple, Becca and Anthony, who lived next door to them. As soon as she had her feet under her at her new job, she vowed to reach out and invite them all over for drinks. She needed to practice forging new relationships, something she'd been hesitant to do since graduating high school. It was time to leave the past behind. No one here knew her secret.

Her stomach fluttered in anticipation as she made the

fifteen-minute commute to the high-rise downtown office building where she'd been hired on as a paralegal for a hard-hitting, private defense attorney. She couldn't help feeling just a little intimidated as she pulled into the underground parking lot and searched for a spot among the fleet of Mercedes and BMWs. After reapplying her lip gloss, she took a deep affirming breath before climbing out of her car. Walking toward the elevator, she fell into step with a young woman she'd met on the day of her interview.

"Hi! Natalie, isn't it?" Haley said, conjuring up a warm smile to quash the acrobatics playing out in her stomach.

"Impressive memory." Natalie grinned. "I didn't hear a word anyone said to me the day I was hired on. I was shaking so hard it all went in one ear and back out the other."

Haley laughed. "I have a pretty good memory for names."

Natalie pressed the button on the elevator. "So, you're going to be working for Nick Wetherington."

Haley shot her a look, elevating one brow slightly. "Do I detect a hint of reservation?"

Natalie twisted her lips. "He's all right, I guess, just a bit demanding."

"Aren't all attorneys?" Haley said with a nervous chuckle, as the elevator doors opened.

She followed Natalie through gleaming glass doors into the opulent law office she'd interviewed in only two weeks earlier. They set their purses on their desks before making their way to the lounge to grab coffees. After agonizing over her outfit for her first day on the job, Haley had settled on a champagne-colored twinset and a black pencil skirt, but in the presence of a sea of expensive suits, she felt seriously underdressed. The lawyers were impeccably groomed; the women expertly made up and coiffed, the men well-turned out in tailored shirts and designer cufflinks. One of the female lawyers threw a scant glance over Haley's outfit, while a couple of the men cast lingering glances over her figure. At five-foot-eleven, she was used to her long, toned legs attracting a fair amount of attention. Looks had been an important membership requirement for the quad squad—another sad reflection of how shallow they'd been back then. Spending time with underprivileged kids in the intervening years had changed Haley's perspective on a lot of things, but it could never change what she'd done.

Armed with an espresso, she returned to her station, eager to begin her day. She idly flipped open the lone case file lying on her desk and began to read.

"Diving right in. That's the kind of work ethic I like to see," a deep voice said.

She glanced up to see her new boss, Nick Wetherington, approaching her, his smoky-brown eyes appraising her. He was even better looking than she'd remembered—she'd been too fraught with nerves the day of her interview to fully appreciate his tall, lean physique, olive skin, and thick, salt-and-pepper hair.

"I can't wait to get started," she said. "Point me in the right direction."

Nick nodded, a furrow of concentration forming on his forehead. "I need you to research the applicable laws for this case and then draft a preliminary report so we can begin preparing for trial." He raised his brows a fraction, as if waiting for her to confirm that she understood.

Haley flashed a smile. "Got it."

"Good." Nick glanced at his Patek Philippe watch. "We'll go to lunch at noon. I'll go over my expectations in more detail then."

"Sounds great," Haley replied, her smile fading as he strode off. She twisted her pen between her fingers pondering Natalie's comment about Nick being a demanding boss. It was an incredible opportunity to be taken under the wing of such an accomplished attorney. She only hoped she didn't prove to be a disappointment to him.

Deeply engrossed in her work, she jolted in her seat when her desk phone rang shortly after eleven. She glanced at it, expecting it to be Nick summoning her to his office, but it was an outside line. Snatching up the handset, she took a quick breath in anticipation of her first client. "Haley Burrows speaking." She pressed the phone tighter to her ear and waited for the caller to respond. The silence on the other end of the line dragged on, crossing into the awkward phase.

"Hello?" Haley said, frowning. "Hello, can you hear me?"

Natalie looked up from her work and glanced quizzically across at her.

Haley pulled a face and shrugged. She waited another moment or two and then replaced the handset in its cradle. "Probably a wrong number," she remarked, unable to keep the tremor from her voice.

She reached for a sheaf of papers and pretended to be absorbed in the contents, trying desperately to keep her fingers from shaking. It couldn't be a coincidence. It was happening all over again.

2

*H*aley spent the rest of the morning distracted, her eyes flicking every few minutes to the phone on her desk, dreading the moment it would ring again. It had all started a couple of months ago at her previous job, the occasional hang-up once or twice a week, quickly escalating to daily incidents. And the worst part about it was that it wasn't limited to phone stalking. More than once, she'd sensed eyes on her, someone watching her as she made her way to her car after work or into her house late at night. She'd suspected every one of her colleagues at one point or another, her paranoia only increasing as time went on. For that reason, she'd kept her distance from her co-workers, not wanting to unwittingly forge a friendship with a creep. Despite her best efforts, she'd never been able to pinpoint who was behind the harassment. She'd been eagerly anticipating the prospect of starting this new job at Huntington and Dodd—hopeful that the sicko who'd been messing with her wouldn't bother her anymore. But it seemed he or she—most likely a male—was a lot more resourceful than she'd reckoned on. He'd already managed to track her down at her new place of work and was doggedly continuing his campaign of terror.

Haley glanced up as Nick strode toward her desk.

"Let's take an early lunch," he said, adjusting the cuff of his sleeve. "I have an important client meeting this afternoon, and I need to get back to prepare my notes."

"Of course." Haley grabbed her purse and followed him out the door, quashing all thoughts of her stalker for the time being. She couldn't help but feel a certain thrill in her gut when Nick swerved past her Toyota 4Runner and peeled out of the underground parking lot in his black Mercedes coupe. Everything about the man screamed power. Under his tute-lage she could make the kind of strides in her career that she aspired to. It wasn't so much the money that came with his job she was after, it was the leverage to do something for the causes she cared about that motivated her. The chance to make amends for her past, to make a stand for victims. As they drove, Nick quizzed her on her family and where she'd gone to school. Haley kept her answers brief, expertly steering the conversation around to his most prestigious cases, guessing correctly that he enjoyed expounding on how he'd won them. She let out a silent sigh of relief as he rattled on. She'd grown accustomed to deflecting questions that pried too much into her past. It was a phase of her life best forgotten.

They dined at an expensive downtown Italian restaurant which Nick obviously frequented, judging by the fact that they were whisked to a table ahead of everyone else standing patiently in line to be seated.

One of the wait staff approached with a carafe of water but Nick waved it away with a flick of his fingers. "Bring us a large bottle of Pellegrino." He fixed a quizzical gaze on Haley. "So, how was your first morning?"

"Fascinating," she replied, stifling the memory of the

hang-up that immediately surfaced. "I totally lost myself in that case. When do you need the report by?"

"Have it on my desk by Wednesday."

Haley fought to keep her expression from betraying her shock. She'd assumed she would have at least a week to work on it. The report would require extensive research on the pertinent laws before she could even begin drafting it.

As she opened her mouth to respond, the waiter appeared clutching the menus.

"I'll have the salmon," Nick said, without skipping a beat. He looked pointedly at Haley. "Do you eat fish?"

"Uh, yes." She threw a sideways glance at the menus in the waiter's hand. Salmon wasn't her favorite dish, but maybe now wasn't the best time to mention that. Nick had made it clear that he was short on time.

"Make that two," he said, giving the waiter a dismissive nod before leaning back in his chair. "So, are you originally from Portland?"

Haley twisted her hands together in her lap. "No, I grew up in Chino Hills, California."

"How do you like your new place in Eastmoreland?"

Haley blinked in surprise. She was sure she hadn't mentioned to anyone at the office that she'd moved recently. Nick must have looked up her address in her employee file. "I … love it. How did you know it was new?"

"I did my homework." Nick's eyes bored into her. "I like to know who I'm dealing with and that I can trust them. No potentially damaging secrets. Don't take it personally. Our reputation at Huntington and Dodd is everything in this business. You learn quickly that people aren't always who they say they are. I don't like surprises."

Haley squirmed uncomfortably in her seat. He obviously hadn't dug deep enough to uncover anything incriminating —her secret was safe.

The rest of the meal passed without any further awkward moments, but Haley couldn't help being discomfited by the way Nick had stared at her as if he knew she was hiding something from him. What else had he discovered about her, and her past? No doubt, he made an intimidating adversary in the courtroom, lording over everyone the way he'd dominated lunch. He would be a dangerous enemy—not one she intended to make. Despite her best efforts to keep up a breezy flow of conversation, she breathed out a silent sigh of relief when the waiter appeared with their bill, and Nick reached for his overcoat.

Back at the office, Natalie elevated a brow when Haley sat down at her desk. "On a scale of one to ten, how bad was it?"

Haley pulled a face. "Eleven. You nailed him. Arrogant and domineering."

Natalie gave a satisfied snort. "I've seen him in action enough times to know how ruthless he can be. At least he takes his paralegals out to expensive restaurants. More than my boss ever does for me. He must like you."

Haley had scarcely immersed herself back in her work before her desk phone rang again. Her skin tingled. Bracing herself, she reached for the handset. "Haley Burrows speaking." After a protracted moment of silence, she repeated herself, a little more loudly this time, tapping her nails irritably on the desk in a bid to mask her rising fear.

Natalie glanced across at her, a mildly curious look on her face.

When there was still no response, Haley replaced the receiver somewhat unceremoniously.

"Wrong number, *again*?" Natalie asked.

Haley gave a hollow laugh. "Either that or they chickened out on whatever lawsuit they were hatching."

"It's so rude to just hang up. They could at least do you

the courtesy of explaining themselves," Natalie said, sounding peeved.

Haley shrugged in an attempt to make light of the situation as she turned her attention back to her computer screen where she was already drafting her report. Her fingers shook as she resumed typing. Two times on her first day—it wasn't a fluke. Her stalker was sending her a clear message that she hadn't eluded him after all.

When five o'clock rolled around, the other paralegals began packing up for the day. Natalie stood and straightened the papers on her desk. "Ready to get out of here? We can go for a drink or something if you want."

"Can I take a rain check on that?" Haley responded. "Nick needs this report by Wednesday. I'll have to pull out all the stops to get it done on time. I'm going to stick around for another hour or two."

Natalie rolled her eyes. "Don't say I didn't warn you. See you tomorrow."

Gradually, the office cleared out until only Haley remained. She glanced up, irritated, at the sound of a cart being shoved through the door heralding the arrival of the janitor. She gave him a cursory nod and then bent her head over her desk again and tried to ignore him as he went about his work, emptying trash cans and dusting down surfaces. She grimaced, glancing up, when a metal can struck the leg of a desk. His gaze locked with hers, his dark eyes steely beneath shaggy graying brows. "Sorry," he called across to her, raising a beefy hand in apology.

Haley gave a tight smile and then resumed her research. She could sense his gaze on her, but she resisted the temptation to look up again, not wanting to get drawn into conversation. When he reached her desk, he pointed wordlessly to the trashcan at her feet.

"Thank you," she said, handing it to him.

He emptied the contents into the clear, plastic bag on his cart without taking his eyes off her. "You're new."

It was more of a statement than a question, but he stood rooted to the spot, obviously expecting a response. Haley gave a curt nod. "That's right, today's my first day."

His eyes meandered to the laser-engraved name block on her desk. "Welcome to Huntington and Dodd, Haley. I'm Lance."

"Nice to meet you, Lance." She shuffled a few papers on her desk hoping he would take the hint and move on.

After a moment or two, he trundled off and she let out a relieved breath. She finished up her research and then slipped the file into her oversized purse, intending to work on her report some more at home. She rode the elevator down to the deserted parking garage and walked toward her car, unlocking it with the key fob as she approached. An icy shiver crossed her shoulders. Was she being paranoid, or could she feel the weight of watchful eyes on her again?

"You have yourself a good evening, Haley," a voice called out from the shadows.

Startled out of her skin, she spun around to see Lance emptying the trash into a dumpster. She gave a tentative wave and hurriedly clambered into her car. Her heart thumped hard against her ribs as she pulled out of the parking lot. Was it a coincidence that he was emptying the trash right when she was leaving? It was beginning to feel as if there were eyes everywhere.

---

*a*t the end of her first week at work, Haley accompanied Natalie to a chic cocktail parlor within easy walking distance of the office. She was determined to make an effort to accept the hand of friendship Natalie had extended. So far, she'd managed to avoid any awkward questions dating back to her high school days, and she'd explained away her apparent lack of a friendship circle by her recent move to a new neighborhood.

Comfortably seated in the bar's elegant lounge area that boasted a panoramic view of the city, Natalie raised her martini glass and clinked it to Haley's. "Here's to surviving your first week under Nick's iron fist."

Haley laughed. "And to getting my first major report in on time. I wouldn't be sitting here right now if I'd goofed that up."

"He interviewed a lot of applicants for that position before he settled on you, you know," Natalie remarked. "Working for Nick Wetherington will give your resume a huge boost, if you can handle the heat, that is."

Haley reached for her drink, thrown off by the subtle

edge to Natalie's tone. She couldn't help but wonder if Natalie had applied for the position and been turned down. Best not to delve too deep into that subject. The last thing she wanted to do was jeopardize their fledgling friendship on their first night out. She raised her glass in another toast. "I'll drink to giving it my best shot."

Natalie took a small sip of her martini and let out a satisfied sigh as her eyes wandered around the pulsating lounge. "Don't look now, but there's a hot dude at the bar checking you out."

Haley resisted the temptation to sneak a peek for all of ten seconds before turning her head slightly and scanning the patrons seated at the bar. A dark-haired man in a well-cut suit caught her eye and raised his tumbler to her. Her stomach fluttered. He was attractive, a little older than her—mid to late thirties if she had to guess.

Haley averted her eyes and stirred her martini with a speared olive. The last thing on her mind right now was dating and she didn't want to give him the wrong impression.

"So, what's the verdict?" Natalie simpered. "Loser, narcissist, one-night stand wannabe, or the ever-elusive husband material?"

Haley gave a good-humored shrug. "None of those options interest me."

Natalie tossed her long blonde hair over one shoulder and cast another furtive look at the bar. "If he is single, he didn't bring a friend with him, so that leaves me out in the cold. I say we forget him and concentrate on our martinis."

"Fine with me," Haley said. "I'm not looking for a relationship. I take it you're not dating anyone at the moment?"

Natalie twirled the stem of her glass between her thumb and forefinger. "I was engaged up until a couple of months ago when I found out my fiancé was cheating on me. It's been hard to throw myself back into the dating arena after spending the better part of a year wading through bridal magazines and vetting potential wedding venues."

"I'm so sorry," Haley said. "That sucks."

Natalie nodded, her eyes clouding over. "The hardest part was that he cheated on me with my best friend—I've known her since kindergarten. I don't understand how they can live with themselves after what they did."

Haley gripped her glass a little tighter, the music blending with the blood suddenly thrumming in her ears. She was an expert in that particular field—learning to live with what you'd done. What other choice did you have when you couldn't go back and put things right?

She swirled her drink gently inside her glass. "Are they still an item—your ex and her?"

"Yeah, they moved in together a few weeks later." Natalie took a hasty gulp of her martini. "But we're not here to dredge up my past. We're here to celebrate your future."

"And yours," Haley added. "At least you found out what your fiancé was really like before you married him."

"I'm trying to look at it that way," Natalie said with a rueful grin. "It sucks being betrayed by someone you trust. It's like they put your heart through a paper shredder."

A shudder crossed Haley's shoulders. Emma had trusted her all along—never suspecting the truth until it was too late. She pasted on a sympathetic smile as she reached for her glass.

"Anyway, enough of that depressing topic," Natalie said.

They ordered another round of drinks and, while they waited for them to arrive, Natalie slipped off to use the restroom. Haley was staring at the dregs in her glass wondering how her stalker had found out where she was working, when a male voice startled her.

"Did your friend ditch you?"

She looked up to see the man who'd been seated at the bar earlier standing by her table. He flipped her a teasing smile and, despite her usual caution around strangers, she grinned back. "No, just taking a bathroom break."

"Bummer. I was hoping to take her seat, but I don't want to crash your party." He fished a card out of his pocket and placed it on the table next to Haley's martini glass, briefly brushing her fingers with his own. "Maybe you and I can have a drink some other time." He winked and walked away without waiting on her response.

Haley picked up the card and studied it. *Jake Wilder, Financial Advisor.* She had to admit, he was cute, but she wasn't about to call a stranger who'd given her his number on a whim—picking up guys in bars wasn't her style. Besides, her stalker knew where she worked, even followed her at times—and they weren't far from the office now. What if it was him?

Natalie returned a moment later, interrupting her thoughts. She plopped herself back down in her seat and reached for her drink. "Did I miss anything?"

Haley slid the card across the table to her. "That guy at the bar stopped by and asked me out for a drink."

Natalie's eyes widened. "I knew it!" She picked up the card and scrutinized it, then cast a casual glance over her shoulder. "Looks like he's gone now. Did you scare him off?"

Haley chuckled. "Not intentionally, but I didn't encourage him either."

"Playing it cool. I like your style." Natalie grinned across the table at her. "I'm glad you came to work at Huntington and Dodd. I've got a feeling we're going to be good friends."

Haley forced a stiff smile as she reached for her drink, the words ricocheting around inside her head.

We're going to be good friends.

That's exactly what the quads had told Emma Murray and

nothing could have been further from the truth. Haley fought to keep her expression cordial. If Natalie knew just how terrible a friend Haley had been in the past, she'd think twice before inviting her into her life.

They chatted some more as they finished their drinks, and then booked Uber rides home, electing to leave their cars in Huntington and Dodd's underground parking garage.

"We have access all weekend," Natalie explained. "You can leave your car there until Monday if you want."

Natalie's ride arrived first, and she climbed in and waved goodnight. "Thanks for a great evening. I had a blast."

Haley stuffed her hands into her pockets to keep warm as she waited for her ride to arrive. Her eyes flitted around, taking in her surroundings. All at once, the hairs on the back of her neck prickled. She had the strangest feeling someone was watching her. Turning slowly, she peered over her shoulder in both directions. No one seemed to be paying her any attention, and there was no sign of anyone huddled in the dark alcove outside the bar. She was probably imagining things—spooked by the hang-ups earlier in the week. She shivered and rubbed her arms vigorously, forcing herself to ignore her irrational fears. Moments later, her ride pulled up and she clambered in gratefully, suddenly longing to crawl into the safety of her bed and go to sleep. Despite an enjoyable evening, and a successful first week working for a taxing boss, her paranoia had a bad habit of putting a damper on everything.

When the Uber driver pulled up outside her house, the young man tipped his head to her. "You have yourself a good one."

"Thanks, you too," Haley replied. She pulled out her keys and stomped up the path to her front door. It was almost midnight. The cul-de-sac was draped in darkness and deathly still. A foreboding shiver crossed her shoulders. As she turned her key in the lock, a curtain twitched in the window of her neighbor's house to the right. She could just about make out a man's pale, wrinkled face peeking out from behind the curtain.

She dismissed a flicker of irritation and, opting to be gracious, gave a reassuring wave in his direction. If the recluse next door wanted to watch his new neighbor coming and going, so be it. At least he was harmless.

---

4

*H*aley ate a lazy breakfast in her recliner in front of the TV on Saturday morning, and then decided to bike into town to pick up her car. She could use the exercise after not making it to the gym all week, and the promise of blue sky peeking through a frothy veil of clouds was too much to resist.

She relished every minute of the ten-mile bike ride, her muscles responding as she pushed herself to her limits in the crisp, morning air. When she reached the entrance to the underground parking lot at Huntington and Dodd, she leaned back on her seat and wiped the sweat from her brow as she freewheeled down to the lower level, endorphins pulsing. The structure was deserted except for her car. Natalie must have been out and about bright and early and picked up her vehicle already. Haley unlocked the back door of her 4Runner and lifted in her bike. She cast a quick glance around, half-afraid Lance would emerge from the shadows with his cleaning cart again, but she quickly dismissed the thought. It was unlikely the janitor worked on weekends.

After climbing into her car, she pulled up a list of local

grocery stores on her phone. She might as well stock up while she was out and about—there hadn't been time to get anything done during the week with all the work she'd brought home to keep up with Nick's relentless demands. She plugged in the coordinates for a nearby Albertsons, started up her car and exited the parking garage.

Inside the grocery store, she pushed her cart up and down the aisles, trying to decide on some easy meals she could throw together in a hurry. If her first week was anything to go by, she could pretty much count on being home late every evening.

She was deep in concentration in the dairy aisle when a vaguely familiar voice said, "I recommend the Icelandic yogurts. Not too sugary."

Haley twirled around and found herself looking directly at Jake Wilder. He was dressed casually in faded jeans and a tight-fitting, long-sleeved T-shirt. She couldn't help but notice how buff his upper body was, a fact that hadn't been so obvious in his jacket the other night at the bar. Suddenly aware that her face was still glistening with sweat from her workout, not to mention the fact that she was dressed in ratty bike shorts and desperately needed a shower, she stammered, "Thanks, but I'm not a fan of yogurt."

Jake raised an eyebrow. "What do you like to eat for breakfast? You don't strike me as a bacon-and-eggs-type girl."

Haley gave a hesitant grin. "Eggs, yes, bacon not so much. I'm as close to a vegetarian as you can get."

A smile played on Jake's lips. "I know a great vegetarian restaurant not far from here, The Raw Vedge." He gestured to the groceries in her cart. "Maybe I can take you to dinner tonight and save you the trouble of chopping up all those vegetables."

Haley hesitated before responding. Was it just a coincidence that they'd bumped into one another again so soon? The disturbing phone hang ups flashed to mind, but she quickly quashed the thought. Jake was hardly the stalker type, and besides, they would be in a public place if they went out to dinner. Perhaps it was time to seize the moment. Her life right now was all about new beginnings. A new home, new job, new friend, maybe even the possibility of a new relationship. She couldn't allow her insecurities to rob her of life going forward. "Sure, why not?" she heard herself say, throwing caution to the wind. "I'll meet you there, say at seven?"

"Great, I'll make a reservation." Jake winked and walked off swinging his basket.

Haley turned her attention back to the dairy products. Her face felt flushed and her heart was beating erratically, and not from the bike ride. She picked up a tub of sour cream and searched for the sell-by date, doubts immediately assailing her. What had she just agreed to? Was she really ready for this? Didn't she have enough on her plate without jumping into a brand-new relationship? And wasn't Jake too old for her, anyway? But, she reasoned, it was only dinner. She didn't have to see him again after that if she didn't want to.

She finished up her shopping and went through the self-checkout, bagging her groceries as she mused over her upcoming date. A small smile tugged at her lips as she pushed her cart across the parking lot. She had to admit she found Jake Wilder intriguing. She plunged her hand into her jacket pocket, pulled out her car key and froze, her eyes riveted on the passenger door. She could scarcely believe what she was seeing. In a daze, she traced a finger across it, hoping it wasn't real, but the rough surface confirmed her fears. Someone had scratched the word, *run*, across the white panel.

She stared at it for several minutes, her stomach churning as she tried to figure out what it meant. Run from what? Was this a random act of vandalism? Some teenagers who'd seen her walking into the store in her workout clothes and thought it would be funny to deface her car? Or was it more ominous than that—a warning of some kind from her stalker? She darted a glance all around the parking lot, searching for possible suspects among the elderly couple making the long hobble arm-in-arm to the grocery store doors, the squawking toddler heartily resisting being strapped into a cart, and a young hippie couple unloading their recyclable bags filled with groceries into the trunk of their Ford Fusion. An unlikely bunch of vandals.

Her brain whirred as she tried to make sense of it. Could it have happened in Huntington and Dodd's underground parking structure? She tried to think back, wondering if she'd even have noticed the damage on the passenger door earlier. She'd walked around the driver's side to load her bike in the back, and then hurriedly climbed in, half-afraid Lance might trudge into view with his cleaning cart in tow.

Her euphoric mood plummeted a few degrees as she loaded her groceries. She got in and fastened her seatbelt, resigned to the fact that she'd have to head to the body shop as soon as she dropped off her groceries at the house. It wasn't how she'd planned to spend her afternoon, but she couldn't drive her car to work in this condition and park it next to Nick's Mercedes on Monday. After all, Huntington and Dodd had a reputation to preserve, as he'd made very clear. And a stalker who knew where she worked might be a surprise Nick was not willing to tolerate.

Back at her house, she put away her groceries before Googling body shops in the vicinity. She called the one with the best reviews and explained to the woman who answered the phone what had happened.

"We aren't open for repairs on Saturdays, only estimates," the woman told her. "If you want us to do the work, you'll have to leave the car with us until Monday."

After Haley hung up, she called a rental car agency and arranged for a vehicle to be dropped off at the body shop. She simply wanted to get this over and done with. She'd have to dip into her savings to take care of the damage, but it was better than involving the insurance company and having her rates jacked up. Committed to her course of action, she climbed back in her car and drove to the body shop.

"Unfortunately, they've keyed it down to the metal," the estimator commented. She ran her fingers over the damage and then made a few notes on her iPad. "What year's your car?"

"It's a 2015," Haley replied. "I bought it new. It was in perfect condition until this happened."

The estimator made a sympathetic sound. "Probably kids. It was obviously done in a hurry."

"Yeah, I figured as much. I left it in an underground parking garage overnight. Not a smart thing to do downtown."

"Let's go inside, and I'll get this paperwork printed out for you," the estimator said.

Haley swallowed when she saw the final total. Could it really cost fifteen-hundred dollars to get rid of three letters? With a resigned flourish of her pen, she signed her name to the work order and pushed it back across the counter just as the rental car pulled up outside.

"How long will it take?" she asked.

"I managed to squeeze you into our schedule on Monday," the estimator said. "We'll call you when it's ready, but I'm guessing it will be around four o'clock or so. We close at five."

"I just started a new job. I doubt I'll be able to get off that early to pick it up."

"Not a problem. You can take care of the payment now. I'll make a note of the gate code on your estimate so you can get in to our parking lot after hours."

"Great, thanks," Haley responded, handing over her credit card.

Forty-five minutes later, she pulled into her driveway in the rental car. She suppressed a grimace when the curtain next door twitched. This time it was a woman's face peeking out, frowning at the strange vehicle. Haley looked away. Was she supposed to wave at her nosy neighbors every time to reassure them it was her arriving home, or should she simply ignore them? She turned off the engine and sat in the car for a moment, debating what to do. On a whim, she decided to go next door and introduce herself. Now was as good a time as any to break the ice.

Before she could talk herself out of it, she got out, walked across the lawn and rang her neighbor's doorbell. After waiting for what seemed like an eternity, she heard shuffling on the other side. The door creaked open a couple of inches and an elderly woman with fluffy white hair and paper-thin, blue-veined skin peered nervously through the crack. She was scarcely five foot, if that.

"Hi," Haley said brightly. "I wanted to introduce myself. I'm your new neighbor, Haley Burrows."

The woman's beady eyes looked her up and down from behind thick glasses. "Edith Moore."

Haley waited a moment for the woman to open the door fully. When she didn't oblige, Haley plowed valiantly on, "Have you lived here long?"

"Twenty-eight years."

"Oh wow!" Haley wracked her brains for something more to say. This was proving far more awkward than she'd antici-pated. Edith obviously wasn't interested in initiating any conversation. If anything, she seemed to be waiting for Haley to leave.

"I saw your husband at the window the other evening," Haley said. "What's his name?"

Edith blinked and wet her lips in a nervous fashion. "That was my brother, Harold."

Haley raised her brows. "I'm sorry, I just assumed you were married."

Edith nodded, as if accepting her apology, but didn't elaborate.

"I should get going," Haley said. "Feel free to pop over anytime for a cup of coffee. Or let me know if I can help with anything. I'm only a doorbell away."

Edith pressed her lips into a tight line and closed the door without another word.

Haley trudged back up her driveway and stuck her key in the front door. The day had started out on a high, but between the senseless vandalism on her car and the icy reception next door, things were rapidly going downhill. Another sliver of paranoia fingered its way into her mind. She hoped she hadn't made a mistake by accepting the dinner invitation tonight from Jake. After all, he was a stranger, and someone was stalking her.

---

5

*H*aley arrived fifteen minutes early at The Raw Vedge so she could observe Jake as he walked in. She shifted in her seat, wondering if he was as nervous as she was. Would he have the same idea as her and arrive early, or stroll in a few minutes late? She picked up her water and took a long sip, trying to calm her nerves. Yes, she was definitely attracted to him. But there was another more ominous reason she wanted to watch him arrive.

A niggling doubt that he'd bumped into her unintentionally at the store was bothering her. As ridiculous as it sounded, she needed to rule out the possibility that Jake Wilder was her stalker. She wanted an opportunity to catch him unawares and observe his mannerisms. You could tell a lot about a person when they were oblivious to the fact that they were being watched. Together with Lachlan, Tina and Vivian, Haley had spent a fair amount of time studying people, homing in on their victims, singling out the weakest from the pack like predators do. Pretty little Emma Murray had been insecure and desperately shy, which was why what they'd done to her was all the more despicable.

Haley's questions about Jake were promptly answered when he appeared at the hostess station five minutes early and brimming with an air of easy self-assurance. He exchanged some banter with the hostess and then glanced across the restaurant to the table where she was seated. His face broke into a smile as he made his way toward her, instantly melting away her paranoia. His forthright manner didn't fit the profile of a crazed stalker. She was equally thankful he hadn't arrived with an armful of flowers in an over-the-top gesture hinting at where he hoped their relationship might be headed. It would take a while to build her trust. Instead, he slid into the booth opposite her with a chuckle. "You're punctual and you clean up good. That's two stars right off the bat."

She laughed in return. "I didn't envision running into anyone I knew at the grocery store or I'd have showered first."

Jake shrugged. "Well, you don't really know me, so you get a pass this time."

Haley rested her chin in her hands. "Why don't you tell me a little bit about yourself?"

Jake leaned back and raised his hands in front of him in mock protest. "Dispense with all the small talk, why don't we? All right, I'll volunteer my vital statistics first and then it's your turn. Let's get the awkwardness over and done with. I'm a financial advisor, thirty-four years old, a self-confessed germaphobe, and never married."

"I had you pegged as late thirties, my bad." Haley tweaked an apologetic grin, secretly thrilled that he was younger than she'd estimated. "Any siblings?"

"Only child." He took a deep breath and looked away for a moment. A dark flicker crossed his face. "My parents died in a car crash in Switzerland eighteen months ago." He hesitated, a tiny furrow forming on his brow. "They were on vacation, celebrating their fortieth wedding anniversary. I don't like to think about it, much less talk about it."

"Wow! That's rough. I'm sorry," Haley said, averting her gaze briefly from the pain pooling in Jake's eyes. He'd obviously been close to his parents.

"What about you?" he asked, reaching for the water carafe.

"I'm an only child too, so I can relate. Twenty-eight and single. My parents live in Florida. They're retired and doing the boating thing, getting all tanned and wrinkled along with other like-minded retirees."

Jake laughed and Haley felt herself relaxing in his company. Before she could ask him anything else, the waiter appeared with the menus. Jake perused the wine list. "What's your preference?"

Haley couldn't help comparing his considerate attitude to Nick's domineering one. Another plus for Jake in her book.

"If you mean red or white, I prefer red," she said.

Jake looked amused. "That's a start. I was thinking more along the lines of full bodied, fruity, or with a hint of aromatic spice."

She arched a teasing brow. "Are you a connoisseur or something?"

He tilted his head to one side. "I enjoy analyzing things. Wine's no exception."

"I hope you're not going to analyze me," she said in a flirting tone.

A slow smile spread across his lips. "I've already begun and so far I like what I see."

Butterflies fluttered in Haley's stomach. The date had only just got underway, but something told her she was going to fall for Jake Wilder, and fall hard.

The food when it came was delicious, and the conversation flowed as smoothly as the excellent Syrah Jake selected. As the evening progressed, and Haley's head began to spin from the wine, she went from vacillating about accepting an invitation for a second date to deciding that she was most definitely smitten. Judging by the way Jake was interlacing his fingers with hers across the table, he felt the same way. Hard as it was to believe, she might have met her dream guy at the same time as landing her dream job, and shortly after purchasing her dream house.

"So, what did you do after you stocked up on eggs this morning at the grocery store?" Jake asked, his eyes twinkling.

Haley twisted her lips, a jarring memory instantly marring the moment. "Actually, I had a nasty surprise when I went back out to the parking lot. Some punk scratched the passenger door of my car all the way down to the metal."

"That sucks." Jake frowned. "What makes you think it was deliberate? It could have been a shopping cart or something."

Haley took a sip of her wine. "Shopping carts can't spell. Someone etched the word *run* in the door. They probably saw me in my workout clothes and thought it would be funny."

A concerned look flitted across Jake's face. "Hard to believe they managed to pull that off in broad daylight without being spotted."

Haley twirled a strand of hair around her finger. "I wondered about that too. I left my car in my company's underground parking lot downtown last night. It's possible it happened there." She paused before adding, "If that's the case, *run* might mean something else."

Jake threw her a curious look. "What do you mean?"

Haley gave an offhand shrug, debating how much to divulge. She wasn't comfortable telling him about the phone hang-ups yet. It was a bit much on a first date to admit you had a stalker. "I don't know, maybe it wasn't random. Maybe someone knew it was my car and wanted to scare me."

Jake looked unconvinced. "Probably just some kids taking

advantage of finding your car in an empty parking lot at night."

Haley pondered the idea as she swallowed a bite of her chickpea masala curry. Something told her it wasn't random. Her thoughts drifted to Lance. It was odd that he'd been in the garage emptying out the trash at the exact same time she was leaving. It might be foolish to consider him a suspect, but he did creep her out a little. Maybe she should run her concerns by Jake and see what he made of it. "The thing is, there's this janitor who works at my office and, to be honest, he kind of spooks me a bit—the weird way he stares at me. I left work late the other evening, and he was coincidentally emptying the trash into the dumpster in the parking garage right when I was walking to my car. I'm sure he watched me leave the office, because he was upstairs only a few minutes earlier and I was the last person there. I can't help wondering if it was him who defaced my car."

Jake straightened up, a look of alarm flashing through his eyes. "Have you talked to your colleagues about him?"

Haley wrinkled up her nose. "Not yet. I didn't want to come across as a total wuss the first week at work. Besides, I figured if he was really weird, someone would have warned me about him. Maybe I'm being paranoid."

"I think you should take the initiative and ask around about him just in case," Jake suggested. "If he is a bit off, you should keep your distance. What about asking that girl from your office—the one you were with the other night? You seemed pretty friendly with her."

"Natalie. Yeah, you're right. I'll ask her about him on Monday." Haley took another bite of her food, quashing down the unsettling image of Lance's expressionless eyes fixed on her.

"Did you call your insurance company about the damage?" Jake asked.

"No, I'm going to pay out of pocket to have it repaired. I already dropped my car off at the body shop this afternoon. It should be ready on Monday after work."

"I can drive you over there to pick it up if you want," Jake said.

Haley swallowed a mouthful of wine, contemplating his offer. He seemed like a real gentleman in every way. She felt safe in his company in public, but she still didn't know him well enough yet to climb into his car, not when she had an unidentified stalker harassing her. "Thanks, but I can leave the rental car I'm in at the body shop and they'll pick it up from there."

Haley felt a flutter in her stomach when she saw the momentary disappointment in Jake's eyes. The attraction was obviously mutual.

When the night drew to a close, she didn't resist his good-night kiss. When she opened her eyes, he smiled down at her. "You're perfect," he whispered. "You're so perfect and you don't even know it. This evening was better than I ever imagined it would be."

Haley's stomach knotted. If only he knew how far from perfect she was, but she could never tell him the ugly truth. She didn't want to shatter what they had before it had even begun. "My parents might beg to differ," she quipped. "I doubt yours think you're perfect either!"

Jake drew back, his expression hardening.

"Ugh, I'm so sorry, I totally forgot," Haley hastened to add. "That was incredibly thoughtless of me. I can't even imagine what it's like to lose someone close to you."

Jake's anguished gaze locked with hers. "No, you can't, not until it happens to you."

6

"So, how was the rest of your weekend?" Natalie asked when Haley joined her in the staff lounge on Monday morning.

"A few highs and lows—mostly highs, all things considered," Haley replied, reaching for a paper cup.

Natalie raised her brows, curiosity filling her eyes. "Well, Friday night was a blast. And you got a hot dude's number without as much as a flutter of your eyelashes. So, I take it our night out was one of the high points."

"Absolutely," Haley assured her as she placed her cup beneath the Nespresso spout. "As a matter of fact, I bumped into that guy the next morning in the grocery store."

"No way!" Natalie cried. "Are you sure he wasn't following you?"

Haley gave a nervous laugh, not wanting to admit that the thought had occurred to her. "He probably thought I was following him. I went to a random grocery store near the office on my way home. I'm still finding my way around the area. Anyway, I was standing there with my cart, all sweaty after biking to the garage, and here he comes strolling down the aisle."

"And?" Natalie prodded as she stirred creamer into her coffee. "Did you give him your phone number this time? Or did you just discuss the quality of the vegetables?"

"Even better," Haley responded with a coy grin. "We went out to dinner."

Natalie clapped a dramatic hand to her chest. "Any fireworks?"

"We kissed and we're going out on a second date, so there was definitely some chemistry between us."

"High five!" Natalie said, slapping her palm against Haley's. "Now, I want all the details."

As they walked back to their desks, coffee mugs in hand, Haley filled Natalie in on the date and everything she'd learned about Jake.

"It was obviously meant to be, you're both only children—definitely a sign," Natalie said. "So far your weekend seems to be all highs. What about the lows?"

Haley tugged down the corners of her lips. "That part sucked. When I came out of the grocery store after bumping into Jake, some moron had scratched the word *run* into the passenger door of my car."

Natalie gasped, her eyes widening in shock. "What? That's awful."

"I know, I was really bummed. I'm not even sure it happened at the grocery store. It might have been here in the parking garage on Friday night. It's possible I didn't notice the damage when I picked my car up."

Natalie frowned. "I doubt it happened here. If that were the case, they would have scratched my car too."

Haley fell silent for a moment. She'd forgotten that Natalie's car had also been in the garage overnight. Goosebumps pricked her arms. It appeared the vandalism wasn't random after all. The sinister message had been directed at her. A cold tingle snaked its way down her spine. Whoever had written the note knew her car. She cast a quick glance around the office and then added in a low voice. "To be honest, the janitor here gives me the creeps—the way he stares at me so intensely. When I was leaving the other night, he just happened to be emptying out the trash in the underground parking lot. He scared me half to death. I think he might have watched me leave the office and followed me down there."

"Lance?" Natalie's expression softened. "He's a bit of an oddball, but he's totally harmless. He can be a bit intense at times—socially awkward—but he's a good sort. He'd do anything for you." Her brow furrowed. "You're not suggesting he had something to do with the vandalism, are you?"

"I don't know, I'm speculating on any possibility at this point."

"Did you make a police report?"

Haley shook her head. "I figured it would be pointless. I can't even say for sure when it happened."

"There are cameras in the underground parking lot. If it happened here, the police might be able to identify the person who did it."

Haley rolled her eyes. "Yeah, you know how that goes; someone between five-seven and six-four, dressed in black wearing a balaclava. Could be anyone on the street. Look, I don't want to kick up a fuss my very first week here, I'd rather just forget it."

"Do you need me to follow you after work so you can get your car looked at?" Natalie offered.

"Thanks, but I already took it to a body shop on Saturday. I'm picking it up after work. I'm in a rental right now."

Natalie sipped her coffee and nodded. "Well, I have to

agree with your analysis of your weekend. Mostly highs, with one very sucky part."

"Haley!" Nick called to her from the doorway of his office.

"Talk later," Haley muttered to Natalie.

She left her coffee mug on her desk and made her way to Nick's office.

"I need you to write up a brief for this case," he said, handing her a thick file without as much as a greeting. "Have it on my desk by tomorrow morning."

"I'll jump right on it," Haley replied with a curt nod, pulling the door behind her as she exited his office.

She grimaced as she walked back to her desk, wondering how she would manage to complete the brief in time. Maybe Nick was testing her. Last week he'd given her a scant three days to draft an extensive report. Now, he was expecting her to turn a brief around overnight. To say he was demanding was an understatement. But she wouldn't let it phase her. She would just have to stay late at the office again. The estimator had told her she could pick up her car any time, so if it was midnight before she got to it, so be it.

The hours slipped by quickly as Haley absorbed herself in her work. Instead of going out to lunch, she nibbled on a tuna sandwich at her desk, but she was still the last one in the office that evening when Lance trundled in with his cart. Her body stiffened, despite Natalie's assurances that he was harmless. She gave him a tight smile and then bent her head over her work again, but she couldn't concentrate with him moving around in the room. Gathering up her things, she packed them in her bag, resolving to finish up the brief at home.

"Good night, Lance," she said as she headed toward the glass doors leading out to the foyer and the elevators.

"Have a good one," he called back to her, leaning on his cart and watching her exit the office. She could feel his eyes burning into her back until the elevator doors closed on her. A chill passed over her as she descended to the parking garage. Lance might be harmless, but his fascination with her was unsettling. The elevator doors opened with a whoosh and she strode across the empty garage to the rental car, clicking open the door. She climbed in and turned on the ignition, frowning at the light on the dash indicating that the right rear tire pressure was low. *Typical rental.* Frustrated, she scrolled through her phone for the nearest gas station. Late as it was, she would have to make another stop and fill up the tire with air before she drove to the body shop. It wasn't worth risking getting stuck along the side of the road somewhere this late at night. While her phone searched, hampered by the weak signal in the underground parking structure, she stepped out of the car and walked around to take a look. A groan escaped her lips. The tire was completely flat. She couldn't drive anywhere with it in this condition.

She rubbed her brow as she considered what to do. How hard could it be to change a tire? YouTube could walk her through it, if she could get a strong enough signal to pull it up, but she was unfamiliar with the rental car and didn't know where to begin to look for the jack. Stupidly, she'd let her AAA Roadside Assistance expire—the renewal letter was buried in the stack of mail on her kitchen counter she had yet to process. She chewed on her lip. She could call Natalie. She doubted Natalie had much experience changing tires, but at least she could drive her to the body shop. Jake would probably know how to change a tire, but it felt awkward to ask him after only one date. She didn't want to come across this needy early on in their relationship, if it even was a relationship.

There was nothing else for it but to call the rental company and ask what the protocol was in this situation— maybe they could bail her out. She climbed back into the car and opened the glove box to retrieve the paperwork, almost jumping out of her skin at the heavy thud of approaching footsteps. Heart knocking against her ribs, she looked up to see Lance peering in at her.

She took a quick, calming breath, trying to ignore the roar of her pulse in her ears. "You scared me half to death, Lance."

His face remained an emotionless mask. "Your tire's flat."

"Yes, I know," she snapped, still reeling from shock. "I must have run over a nail or something."

His expression didn't change, despite the scathing tone she'd slipped so easily back into—one the quad squad had expertly wielded on those they looked down on, a tone she loathed herself for using.

"I can change it if you want," Lance said.

Haley gripped the steering wheel with one hand. Part of her wanted to refuse his offer, but another part of her just wanted to get out of here as quickly as possible. Natalie had assured her he was harmless—perhaps she needed to have a little faith that he'd been sent her way to help her. "That would be great," she said, climbing out of the car. "I'm not even sure where the jack is."

Wordlessly, Lance opened the trunk and lifted out a panel exposing the spare tire and the jack. Haley watched him get to work, her shoulders slumped in resignation. She would be indebted to him after this. He struggled to loosen the nuts on the wheel, and she felt bad about putting him to so much trouble, especially after the unreasonable thoughts she'd harbored about him. "I really appreciate your help," she said. "I need to drive to the body shop and pick up my own car after this."

"Fender bender?" Lance asked without looking up.

"Not exactly. It needed a little paint job," Haley answered.

"It looked okay to me," Lance remarked. "I thought you kept it real nice."

"I try to." Haley twisted her lips. "Someone keyed my car on the passenger side. I noticed it when I came out of the grocery store last Saturday, but I'm not exactly sure when or where it happened. I left my car here overnight on Friday."

Lance grunted in response. He pulled off the flat tire and replaced it with the spare, securing the wheel nuts with a socket wrench. When he turned to face Haley, his face was grave. "Just for the record, you didn't run over a nail. Your tire was slashed. Looks like someone has it in for you."

7

*H*aley drove to the body shop in a daze, Lance's words echoing around inside her head. *Looks like someone has it in for you.* Fear prickled through her. What if he was right? What if the slashed tire was connected to the damage to her car door? If that was the case, it must have happened in the parking structure at Huntington and Dodd. Surely it couldn't have been someone who worked there, could it? It certainly wasn't Lance—he wouldn't have told her the tire had been slashed if he'd done it. Haley frowned. No one knew she was driving a rental, no one other than Natalie. This had to be the work of hoodlums taking advantage of the fact that cars were being left unattended in the underground parking lot. After all, they'd got away with it the first time.

She made a mental note to ask around in the office tomorrow to see if anyone else's vehicle had been tampered with. Maybe she should ask the property manager if she could review the security camera footage on the off chance the lowlife who'd slashed her tire had neglected to cover his or her face. Reality television had taught her that not all criminals were masterminds.

Still mulling over what had happened, she pulled up to the body shop gate, a spiked wall of iron shrouded in shadows. Despite wanting to believe that what had happened to her car was random vandalism, her instincts told her otherwise. Someone was preying on her. It explained the queasy feeling that came over her at times, as though a stranger's eyes were fastened on her, following her every movement. And then a harrowing thought struck. What if someone had followed her here to the body shop tonight? Her wide-eyed gaze locked on the rearview mirror, but no headlights shone back at her announcing the unwelcome presence of a stranger. Her heart pounded beneath her ribs. She shouldn't have come here alone this late at night. It had been a foolhardy decision. Suddenly spooked at the idea of being alone in the isolated parking lot, she frantically punched in the number the estimator had given her and waited for the gate to trundle open along its rails. She pulled in and drove along the line of cars until she spotted her 4Runner. With a final sweeping glance around the deserted parking lot, she parked the rental, and climbed into her own car.

Once she was safely back on a familiar road, and her heartbeat had slowed to a more natural pace, she called the rental company and left a message explaining what had happened. When she hung up, she dialed her parents' number. She was in sore need of a reassuring voice. It was almost midnight Florida time, but her parents were both night owls, often watching movies until the early hours.

Her mother answered the phone on the second ring. "Hey, honey."

"Hi, Mom." A wave of calm instantly washed over her at the familiar sound of her mother's voice.

"I'm going to put you on speaker so your father can listen

in," her mother said. "How's the new house working out? Everything good?"

"Yes, I love it! I can't thank you enough for helping me out with the down payment."

"What about your new job?" her father chimed in.

"It's going great so far. Busy, but I'm learning a ton."

"I bet you are," her father responded. "Has that overbearing boss of yours settled down any? Not driving you up the wall, I hope?"

"Nick's demanding, but he's one of the top defense attorneys in the district. I'm lucky to be working for him."

"How about your other colleagues?" her mother asked. "Have you made any friends there yet?"

"Yeah, they're a good bunch. There's another girl around my age—Natalie. We get on great. And I met a guy. We've only gone on one date so far, but I really like him. We'll see how it goes."

"Well, you certainly are leading a charmed life, aren't you?" her mother said with a pleased chuckle. "I'm so happy for you, darling. You deserve it after all your hard work."

Charmed might be a stretch. Haley gripped the steering wheel tightly, debating whether or not to tell her parents what was going on. Part of her wanted their reassurance that everything was going to be all right. But another part of her wanted to protect them from worrying needlessly about her.

"Something on your mind, sweetie?" her mother ventured.

Haley gave a wry smile. Nothing slipped past her intuitive-on-steroids mother.

"Nothing major. I had a bit of bad luck with my car this past week."

"Your car?" her father echoed. "Is it not running properly? You are changing the oil regularly, aren't you, Hales?"

She rolled her eyes. "It's not a maintenance issue, Dad. It was vandalism."

"Vandalism!" her mother exclaimed. "Are you okay, dear? Did they break your window or something?"

"I'm fine. I wasn't in the car when it happened. I left it in the parking garage overnight and someone scratched the word *run* into the passenger door," Haley explained. "And then tonight, someone slashed my right rear tire and left me stranded. Luckily the janitor was there and he changed the tire for me." She chewed on her lip, biting back the desire to mention that she found him creepy and had half-suspected he might be behind it.

"Are you working in a dangerous area or something?" her mother asked, her voice rising an octave.

"That's just it, it's not a bad area at all," Haley replied. "Quite the opposite, in fact. Whoever slashed my tire was probably captured on the security cameras. I doubt I'll be able to ID anyone from the footage, but I'm going to talk to the property manager tomorrow and see what he says."

"You need to get down to the police station and make a report first thing in the morning," her father urged. "This should be on file in case it continues."

"Yeah, I suppose," Haley said dubiously. "I don't want to kick up too much of a fuss at my new job in case it was just teenagers. If something else happens, I'll definitely file a report."

"I hope it's not someone from your new company," her mother said.

Haley frowned, contemplating the idea. Other than Lance, she hadn't seriously considered the possibility that someone else from the office had damaged her car. But Natalie had let slip that quite a few people had applied for her position. Had Natalie been one of them? Haley could feel her paranoia weaving its way back into her thoughts. Natalie *had* sounded somewhat disgruntled when she'd mentioned Nick taking Haley out to expensive restaurants. *More than my boss ever does.* Was she secretly harboring resentment? Haley shook the thought free, hating that her paranoia was getting the best of her. Even if Natalie had applied for the job working for Nick, she'd made a point of befriending Haley— she wouldn't have done that if she was jealous of her. Unless she was schizophrenic, it made no sense. Haley didn't know the rest of the staff very well yet. Nick was a bit of a dark horse, and it had struck her as odd that her new boss had made it his business to find out so much about her private life, but he didn't have any reason to wage a campaign of terror against her.

"I mean, it sounds like it only happens in the company parking garage," her mother continued.

"That's true, but the garage is accessible to anyone," Haley explained. "It's an underground parking structure for all the office buildings in the tower."

"Don't they have a security guard on duty?" her father asked.

"No, only the cameras."

"Well, the good news is it doesn't sound like some delusional romantic stalker, which would be a much more dangerous situation," her father observed. "My guess is it's probably some teenage punks. Even so, it would be best if you didn't stay late at the office on your own anymore."

"You're right," Haley agreed. "I'm going to try and avoid that for the next couple of weeks at least until this blows over."

"I just don't understand why people do things like that— hurting others for no good reason," her mother said.

Haley's gut tightened. It was a haunting question. She hadn't had any good reason to hurt Emma Murray, which made her actions all the more abhorrent. Her parents had no idea that she was the one responsible for what had happened —no one knew, other than her quad sisters, and they were equally culpable, they had egged her on. Haley grimaced. Maybe she deserved everything bad that was happening to her. She was reaping what she'd sown.

8

*O*ver the next few weeks, Haley didn't experience any more unsettling hang-ups at work, but she still had the feeling someone was following her at times. She'd been tempted to tell Jake about it now that they were dating regularly, but she was afraid he would think she was being ridiculous. Thankfully, nothing more had happened to her car since the tire-slashing incident. She'd asked the building manager to review the footage, but, coincidentally, it turned out the cameras were malfunctioning at the time. They had since been repaired, but it did little to give Haley any peace of mind. She made a point of not being the last one to leave the office anymore.

On the plus side, she'd been arriving home earlier in the evenings, so she'd finally been able to connect with her new neighbors, and, apart from Edith Moore and her equally reclusive brother, Harold, they were a friendly enough bunch. At least she'd thought so until the morning she'd discovered an envelope containing a note card tucked under her windshield wiper. She'd thrown a harried glance around the cul-de-sac, but no one else was out and about. Hopefully, she hadn't inadvertently parked in a spot one of her neighbors had laid claim to. Edith and Harold seemed like the type to write her a nasty warning rather than having a friendly word with her about it. With a sense of foreboding, she tore open the envelope and scanned the note card inside. Blood drained from her head. She swayed forward, clutching the side of her car for support. The word *die* was scrawled on the card in red Gothic letters, splotches of ink splattered like blood all over. With a muffled shriek, she dropped the card at her feet, her eyes darting around the cul-de-sac to see if anyone was watching from behind a curtain. Her chest heaved up and down for several minutes as she fought to steady her breathing. When she'd regained some measure of composure, she retrieved the card and retreated inside her house, where she tore the note and envelope up and tossed the pieces in the trashcan.

In retrospect, she should have taken it to the police. It was the confirmation she needed that what was happening to her was far from random. Someone was harassing her, and it was clear they knew both where she worked and lived. Now, her misgivings extended to her neighbors—none of whom she knew well enough to rule out as suspects. The new house she'd looked forward to coming home to each evening suddenly seemed less hospitable. Sleep had eluded her lately, and the sleep deprivation wasn't helping her state of mind. She wasn't functioning well at work with a sluggish brain, and she'd given up volunteering entirely in the meantime— her current stressed-out state wasn't beneficial to the kids who deserved better.

A few days after she found the note on her windscreen, she broke down and told Jake everything. He'd been nothing but supportive ever since, checking up on her regularly and making sure she made it to work safely each morning. It was terrifying to think that whoever was stalking her knew where she lived and worked. Everyone in her cul-de-sac, as well as at Huntington and Dodd, had become a suspect in her mind.

Haley considered each of her neighbors in turn, but they had no apparent motive that she was aware of. She racked her brains for other possibilities, but there was no angry ex-boyfriend lurking in the wings. Her previous relationship had ended on amicable terms. She had no enemies that she knew of, which left only the possibility of a stranger, as dark and disturbing as that sounded.

WHEN JAKE PROPOSED four months later, Haley stood there speechless, staring down in awe at the two-carat ring in a black velvet box. They'd hiked to the top of Multnomah Falls one chilly Sunday morning and while Haley was admiring the view, Jake got down on one knee in front of her.

"Haley Burrows, will you do me the honor of becoming my wife?"

She clapped a hand to her lips. "Jake! Are you serious? It's too soon," she protested, her heart booming in her chest, partly from the steep hike they'd just undertaken, partly from the thrill of what was unfolding before her eyes.

"You know I love you, Hales," Jake said, his voice thick with emotion. "You're the one I want to spend the rest of my life with. I want to be with you every day, to love you and protect you. You won't ever have to be scared again—of stalkers, or spiders, or anything else that comes your way."

Haley blinked back tears. For too many years, she'd been wary of getting close to anyone, but her friendship with Natalie had helped break down those barriers. In the end, it hadn't taken Jake long to sweep away any lingering reservations and when she said *yes*, with only the tiniest flicker of hesitation, he quickly slipped the glittering ring on her finger and wrapped her tightly in his arms. "I promise you I'll never let anything happen to you," he whispered in her ear.

Her heart skipped a beat at the fervor in his voice. In all honesty, it was a bit of a whirlwind romance, but Jake was kind, fun, ambitious and attractive—everything Haley wanted in a man. And, now that she had her house and a good job, maybe it was time to leave behind her fears and insecurities and take a chance on love. There was also the fact that Jake made her feel safe, and the truth was that she'd become increasingly nervous living on her own of late.

Natalie was thrilled for her, ogling over her engagement ring, and singing Jake's praises, but her parents were more dubious when she called them to give them the news. They urged her to take her time before rushing into anything. But, Haley reasoned, they hadn't met Jake yet, so it was only natural they would err on the side of caution.

When Jake told her he was shopping for a wedding present for her, Haley shocked him with her response. "Don't bother, I already know what I want—a security system installed in the house."

"That's not very romantic." Jake rumpled his forehead. "I was going to surprise you with some jewelry."

"Save it for our first anniversary. I want to feel secure in my own house. I don't want to have to worry anymore when I lie awake in bed at night."

Jake slid an arm around her. "You don't have anything to be concerned about. Nothing's happened in ages, other than that silly note on your windshield months ago. Probably neighborhood kids running around leaving notes on cars for a laugh."

Haley frowned. "I'm not sure that's all there is to it. Even though nothing's happened in a while, I still feel like some-one's following me at times. Maybe I'm just being paranoid, but I want to feel safe in my own home at least."

Jake tucked a strand of hair behind her ear. "And so you should. If you want a security system, I'll buy you one. But I'm still going to surprise you with something special on our wedding day."

Haley snuggled up to his firm chest and closed her eyes. It was a horrible feeling to think a stranger was watching her, intruding on her world at will. A primal violation of sorts. She was only half-convinced that things would be better once Jake moved in—what could he really do to stop a stalker?

AFTER TALKING THROUGH THEIR OPTIONS, and ruling out a small ceremony in a registrar's office with Haley's parents as their witnesses, they opted to elope. Haley knew if she involved her parents, they'd only try and persuade her to have a big wedding with all the bells and whistles, and she'd no desire for a lavish affair that would require seeing faces from her past she would sooner forget. Besides, Jake had no family to invite anyway. Her parents might be miffed at first, but ultimately they'd come round to the idea. Two months later, Haley and Jake tied the knot on board a private yacht off the coast of San Francisco.

After the ceremony, Jake gave her a gold locket engraved with their wedding date and the word *forever*. Haley clutched it tightly in her hand, drawing strength from the promise it held. With Jake by her side, she'd no longer have to face whatever came her way alone. Maybe now, the creep who'd been messing with her would finally leave her in peace for good.

Despite Haley's parents' disappointment that their only daughter had dispensed with a white wedding, Jake managed to charm them when they talked on the phone after the ocean ceremony. Natalie was somewhat peeved at being excluded from the surprise wedding at first, but when Haley explained that she was trying to be sensitive to the fact that Jake had no family to invite, and that a wedding would only have rubbed salt in the wound, she relented and quizzed Haley for all the details, sobbing when she read the personalized vows they'd exchanged.

After their wedding, they'd spent three days and nights in San Francisco, opting to plan a proper honeymoon later when Haley could get the time off work.

"I almost don't want to go back," she said to Jake as they buckled in for their return flight home. "This is the first time I've felt unafraid in months. I'm scared of what might happen when we go home."

"Nothing's going to happen to you now that we're together," he promised, kissing her softly. "I'll make sure of it."

But something did happen toward the end of her first week back at work—nothing to do with the stalker, and nothing Jake could have prevented from happening.

Nick buzzed her on her desk phone. "I need to see you in my office right away."

Haley got to her feet, mentally running through the possible reasons her boss might want to speak to her urgently. There had been a note of admonition in his voice, but she couldn't figure out what she'd neglected to do, or perhaps not done to his satisfaction.

She stepped into his office a moment later and closed the door behind her, taking a seat opposite him.

He leaned back and pressed his lips together before addressing her. "I'm not sure what you think you're playing at, but I don't appreciate the sentiment."

Haley drew her brows together and stared at him blankly. "I don't understand. What are you talking about?"

Nick let out an exasperated sigh. "Don't make this any worse than it already is. I'm a happily married man. We have a working relationship, nothing more. If I take you to lunch, it's strictly business."

"You've lost me." Haley gave a nervous laugh. "I have no idea what this is about."

Nick narrowed his eyes. "It's one thing to proposition me, it's another thing to deny it."

"Proposition you? You must be mistaken!" Haley protested. "I've never done anything of the sort."

"Then what do you call this email?" Nick retorted, sliding a sheet of paper across the table to her and jabbing at it with his finger.

Perplexed, Haley picked it up and began to read.

Hɪ Nɪᴄᴋ,

These past few months have been everything I hoped they would be, and I've especially enjoyed getting to know you. I love the romantic restaurants you choose for our intimate lunches. You've probably realized by now that I've developed feelings for you. I can tell by the way you look at me that you desire me too. It's nothing to be ashamed of. People meet and fall in love at work all the time. I just want you to know that whenever you're ready, I'll be waiting. You won't be disappointed.

Truly yours,
Haley
xoxo

Sʜᴇ ʟᴏᴏᴋᴇᴅ ᴜᴘ, her chest seizing, the atmosphere in the room suddenly stifling as her face flushed. "I didn't write this, Nick. You have to believe me. I don't know where this came from, but it certainly didn't come from me."

Nick shook his head in disbelief. "It came from your email account. Are you trying to tell me one of your colleagues sent it as a joke? This is a law firm of professionals."

Haley opened and shut her mouth a couple of times before setting the paper back down on the desk. "I don't know who was behind it, but all I can tell you is that I would never write something like this. You're not the only one who's happily married. I just got back from my honeymoon in case you've forgotten. And why would I sabotage a job I love?"

Nick studied her with a contemplative air for a moment, before exhaling loudly and reaching for the paper. He swiftly scrunched it up and tossed it in the trashcan. "All right, I'm willing to let it go this once. I'll put it down to some kind of lowlife office prank. We'll leave it at that so don't discuss it any further—I don't want everyone getting wind of it. In the meantime, you might want to think about changing the password on your computer."

Haley nodded as she got to her feet. "Of course." Her legs felt like jelly as she exited Nick's office. She kept her gaze down as she made her way back to her desk, not wanting to catch anyone's eye—not wanting anyone to read the shock on her face. Who could have done this? It was obviously some kind of practical joke, but it was in very poor taste. She desperately wanted to run it by Natalie so she could pick her brain. Natalie had worked here a lot longer than she had, and she knew the scoop on everyone. But Nick had made it clear he didn't want her discussing the unsavory email with anyone. And she'd given him her word.

Unsettled, she found herself casting furtive glances at everyone as they went by, weighing the possibility that one of her colleagues was behind the email. Was it connected to the other things that had happened to her? If that was the case, someone at Huntington and Dodd was definitely involved. When five o'clock finally rolled around, she packed up her bag, grateful to be leaving the oppressive atmosphere of the office behind.

"How'd your day go, sweetheart?" Jake asked when she arrived home.

"It sucked, to be honest with you," she answered, pulling out a bar stool at the kitchen counter where he was uncorking a bottle of red wine.

"Why? What happened?" He poured her a glass and handed it to her.

"I'm not really supposed to talk about it. Nick asked me not to."

Jake raised his brows. "I'm your husband. It's not like I'm going to tell anyone. I'm sure Nick meant not to talk about it at the office."

Haley sipped her wine. "Okay, but you'd better not breathe a word about it. If it gets back to the office, I'll be fired on the spot." She hesitated, her stomach roiling. "Someone sent Nick an email from my account—all about my feelings for him and asking him if he felt the same way, basically propositioning him to start an affair."

Jake looked momentarily stunned. He set down his wine glass and ran his fingers through his hair. "Who would do something like that? It sounds petty for a bunch of lawyers and paralegals—more like a high school prank."

"That's just it. I can't imagine anyone at the office doing something so stupid. But it must have been someone at work. No one else had access to my computer. Maybe it was someone who wanted my job—Natalie told me Nick interviewed several internal applicants."

Jake thought for a minute. "I might be able to find out who it was if I could get on your computer."

Haley set down her glass, her shoulders slumping. "Nick was adamant he didn't want me telling anyone about it. He's not going to let a stranger walk into the office and access my work computer."

"I could go in after hours," Jake offered.

"That's against company policy—you're not an employee," Haley said. "And you'd be on camera, so I'd risk losing my job. Isn't there some way you can access my computer remotely?"

Jake rubbed his chin. "I'm not that computer savvy. And I imagine Huntington and Dodd doesn't skimp on their security protocol."

Haley swatted her hand through the air. "I just want to forget about it. I'm going to do as Nick says and write it off as a stupid practical joke. If it happens again, we'll talk about how I can find out who's trying to sabotage my career."

Jake leaned over and kissed her forehead. "Sounds like a plan. I'll drink to that."

Haley got to her feet. "I'm starving. How about I make us a vegetable stir fry?"

"Perfect. I'll set the table."

Haley slid out the drawer containing her pots and pans and rummaged through them looking for her wok. "Did you empty the dishwasher this morning?" she called over her shoulder.

"Yep, I'm way ahead of you," Jake responded, with an elaborate wink.

"That's odd," Haley said, opening and shutting the other cabinets in the kitchen. "I can't find my wok anywhere."

Jake walked over and dug through the pots and pans. "That is strange. I know I put it in here."

Haley pulled out a large frying pan. "It must be around here somewhere. I'll use this for now."

The stir fry wasn't cooked to her satisfaction without her wok, but Jake praised her efforts. "Tastes good to me sautéed in that truffle oil." He cleaned his plate, but Haley pushed hers aside after a few bites, unable to shake a foreboding feeling. It was one of those weird days when nothing seemed to be going quite right, all her fears threatening to resurface. Was it possible the email was connected to the hang-ups and the vandalism, or was she reading too much into it?

"Wanna watch a movie tonight?" Jake asked. "We could find something on Netflix."

Haley shrugged. "Sure, so long as it's a comedy. I need a good laugh after the day I've had."

"I'm going to hit the shower first," Jake said.

"Go ahead. I'll clean up in here."

She scraped the plates into the garbage disposal and turned it on, listening to the familiar sound of the blades spinning and the water draining. After loading the dishes in the dishwasher, she pulled out the trash bag and tied a knot in it before carrying it outside. She was just about to toss the bag into the outdoor garbage can when something caught her eye. Her brain flooded with confusion. What was her wok doing in the trash?

9

*H*aley puzzled over the wok in the garbage can for several days. Jake adamantly denied throwing it out, and they ended up getting into a heated argument about it after he dared to suggest she might have accidentally tossed it out with the trash. All her fears had reignited with a vengeance, her paranoia mushrooming overnight. For the first time, she wondered if it was possible that she was losing her mind, if the stress of her high-powered job and Nick's never-ending demands was finally getting to her. *Could* she have thrown out the wok? Either way, she definitely hadn't sent that email to Nick. Her cheeks burned at the thought. Granted, he was a good-looking man, but she was happily married to Jake—she wasn't spending her days fantasizing about having an affair with her boss.

On the surface, the discarded wok appeared like a harmless enough incident, but it really bothered her. It opened up the possibility that someone had been in their house. One of their neighbors, perhaps? Her thoughts drifted back to the note she'd found on her windscreen. Someone always seemed to know when she was coming and going. And the hang-ups at her first job had begun around the time she'd moved in here. Was there a weirdo living in her cul-de-sac? Following her? Edith next door was odd, but she was hardly the type to go around breaking into other people's houses and leaving threatening messages. Haley had yet to meet Harold—but, by all appearances, he was even more of a recluse than his sister.

She'd engaged in small talk with her other neighbors, but she still hadn't invited them over for drinks. Fear of her unknown stalker had made her disinclined to host them in her home as a single woman. Perhaps now that she was married it would a good time for her and Jake to host a small gathering and get to know their neighbors better. She needed to gain their trust, see if any of them struck her as odd or suspicious. Maybe some of them had experienced unusual things happening to them or to their vehicles. It was time to do some digging and find out if the person trying to scare her out of her wits resided in her cul-de-sac.

At first, Jake was reluctant to jump on board with the idea of hosting a get-together. He was still convinced she'd accidentally tossed out the wok. "It's ridiculous to think any of our neighbors broke in and threw away our wok. Why would they do such a random thing? I don't like the idea of inviting them over with ulterior motives. That makes us the weirdos."

"I'm only asking you to try and get to know them a little better," Haley responded. "Find out if any of them are eccentric, or loners—other than Edith and Harold—or if any of them has experienced weird stuff happening like I have. Someone's messing with me, and I need to know who it is."

"No one's been in our house, Hales. That's why we installed the alarm system," Jake reminded her.

She arched a brow at him. "You mean the one you keep forgetting to set when you leave the house?"

He pulled a sheepish face. "It's only happened once or twice."

Haley let it slide. It irritated her that Jake wasn't as vigilant about setting the alarm as she was, but she didn't want to start an argument. She just wanted to get to the bottom of what was going on, and the sooner the better. Lately, she seemed to be on edge all the time, even snapping at Jake, and she didn't like who she was becoming. "We'll keep it simple," she assured him. "We'll invite them over for dessert and drinks."

Jake threw up his hands. "Do whatever you want. I can see I'm not going to be able to talk you out of this one."

Haley got to work at once making up invitations on her computer, printing them out, and hand delivering them to the mailboxes in the cul-de-sac. Everyone texted affirmative responses over the next day or two, except for Edith and Harold. Haley gave them until Thursday evening and then set off up the pathway to their front door to extend a personal invitation. She rang the doorbell and waited until Edith cracked the door a few inches and squinted out at her.

"Hi, Edith," Haley chirped. "Did you get my invitation to dessert and drinks on Saturday night?"

"I … we don't go out much," Edith replied.

"We're just next door," Haley said. "You don't have to stay long, but it would be lovely to see you."

Edith puckered her forehead and adjusted her glasses. "Indeed."

Haley raised her brows. "Is that a yes, you will stop by?"

Edith blinked uncertainly as she pushed the door closed. "I'll talk it over with Harold."

Haley took a step back and stared at the door that had been slammed in her face. "Suit yourself," she muttered under her breath as she stomped back over to her own house. It hardly mattered if they came or not. Somehow, she doubted they'd been responsible for throwing her wok in the trash—if Edith couldn't even bring herself to stick her head out of her own front door, it was unlikely they'd been trespassing in her house.

The night of the party rolled around, and Haley and Jake put the finishing touches to the array of desserts on the kitchen island. Candles flickered around the counters, and white wine and sparkling cider chilled in a hammered copper ice bucket while several bottles of red wine decanted nearby. Haley had already indulged in a glass to calm her nerves. Just the possibility of coming face-to-face with her stalker was enough to ratchet up her heartbeat.

The doorbell rang a couple of minutes before seven and Haley went to the door. Jim Markham, their other next-door neighbor, stood on the doorstep with a bottle of wine tucked under his arm. "Hope I'm not too early."

Haley beamed at him and took the wine he proffered her. "Not at all, come on in. It's great to see you."

The young couple from across the street, Becca and Anthony, arrived next followed, moments later, by the soccer parents, Liz and Stan. To Haley's relief, they'd left their rambunctious kids at home with a babysitter.

"Couldn't pass up the chance for an adult evening," Stan blustered with an elaborate wink.

Haley chatted for a few minutes with both couples before setting down her glass and excusing herself to make sure Edith and Harold weren't standing awkwardly on the front doorstep. After waiting by the door for a moment or two, she resigned herself to the fact that they weren't going to make an appearance and made her way back to the kitchen. Becca and Liz were deep in conversation, while Jake was holding court with the men who were guffawing at some story he was telling them. Haley joined the two women and retrieved her wine glass from the counter. "I was just making sure

Edith and Harold weren't standing outside," she explained. "I didn't get a commitment from them either way."

Becca and Liz exchanged a dubious look.

"You won't lure those two out of their house unless there's a fire or something," Becca said. "I told Anthony he's going to end up just like them if he doesn't quit gaming."

"They're certified recluses," Liz agreed. "They have their groceries delivered. They only ever leave for the occasional doctor appointment. A taxi picks them up."

"So, you've never had them over to your place either?" Haley asked, taking a sip of her wine. She needed to slow down. For some reason, the alcohol was going to her head more quickly than usual, and tonight, above all nights, she wanted to have her wits about her in order to get a read on her neighbors. Her first impression of Liz and Becca was that they seemed pretty tight. Maybe the two couples socialized together.

Becca took a bite of an eclair and tinkled a laugh. "I've never even been able to draw Edith into the garden for a chat."

"I bet she'd have plenty to chat about," Liz bantered. "She's forever peeking around that curtain of hers checking to see who's coming and going."

Haley silently digested the information. If Edith watched everything that transpired in the cul-de-sac, she might have seen someone entering her house. Haley needed to go back over there and talk to her as soon as she got a chance. Edith might turn out to be her best source to get to the bottom of what was going on.

Haley picked up a platter of desserts and wandered over to the men, feeling increasingly tipsy. "Dig in, we can't let these go to waste."

Jim grinned and loaded up his plate. "I have a single man's appetite when it comes to home baked goods."

"How long have you lived here?" Haley asked.

"Almost four years," Jim replied through a mouthful of cupcake. "I work at the steel plant as a supervisor. The night shift's harder on the married men so I'm kinda stuck with it. Doesn't do much for your social life."

Haley flashed him a sympathetic smile. "I imagine it's hard to sleep during the day."

"I don't need much sleep. I get by on about four hours."

Haley tried to focus, her vision blurring. "What do you do the rest of the time?"

"Odd jobs. I used to be a handyman. And I'm into hunting. Ducks and geese mainly. I don't do big game."

Haley grimaced. "I'm a vegetarian, for the most part. I do like seafood, but even the thought of fishing hurts me on a primal level."

Jim nodded. "I get that a lot. But I love going out into the wild, being alone and one with nature. I'm not one for crowds. And I don't kill anything unless I'm gonna eat it. You might want to try duck sometime, if you haven't already. It makes for good eating. I can bring you over some jerky if you like."

"Well, I'm sure my husband would enjoy it," Haley said, feeling nauseated, but unable to think of a polite way to deflect the offer. Her mind was running a mile a minute, alcohol and paranoia blending as one. Could Jim be her stalker? On all the crime shows she'd ever watched, being a loner was a red flag. If he didn't sleep much, he had plenty of time to follow her around—stalk her even. And he was a hunter after all. He seemed friendly enough, but maybe behind the scenes he was a lonely man with a sick obsession.

Unsettled, she turned her attention to the other men in the group. "So, Stan, do you coach soccer?"

"Yeah, hanging out with the kids on Saturdays keeps me

young, and it makes a change from being stuffed into a suit and tie all week."

"What do you work at?" Haley asked.

"I'm a realtor. In fact, I showed this place before you bought it."

Haley stiffened, clenching the platter in her hand, only too aware that her smile had frozen on her face even as the room began to spin around her.

Did Stan still have a key to her house?

10

---

*H*aley woke the next morning with a blistering headache. Slowly, she forced her eyes open and patted the other side of the bed. The sheets were cold to her touch. Jake must have been up for a while. Scrabbling around for her phone, she squinted at the screen, attempting to read the time. *11:37am.* She gasped in disbelief. How was it possible she'd slept this late? Sinking back on her pillow, she closed her eyes again, trying to remember how the party had ended. Her mind was a complete blank, devoid of any recollection of going to bed. She recalled greeting her neighbors as they arrived, all of them except for Edith and Harold Moore who had failed to show—that much she knew. She distinctly remembered walking around the kitchen refilling wineglasses and offering platters of the bite-sized desserts she'd slaved over for most of yesterday. But, for some reason, she couldn't remember saying goodnight to anyone, or seeing any of her neighbors to the door, or anyone thanking her for the great evening they'd had, come to think of it.

After a few more minutes of willing the painful pounding in her head to end, she gingerly moved aside the duvet and swung her legs to the side of the bed. Stumbling into the bathroom, she stared critically in the mirror at her drawn face, shocked at the dark circles under her eyes. She looked like a train wreck. She desperately needed a shower, but that would have to wait. The first thing on her agenda was a mug of strong coffee to try and jolt her short-term memory into action. She grabbed some Advil and swallowed them down with a palmful of water before exiting the bathroom, feeling weak and disjointed.

Hesitantly, she made her way downstairs. Jake was seated at the kitchen island scrolling through his iPad. He barely glanced up when she walked in.

"Morning," she offered, with more gusto than she felt.

"Hey."

Despite the throbbing in Haley's head commanding her attention, it was impossible to miss the air of hostility emanating from him. She wet her lips, racking her brain for some memory of what had brought it about. Had they argued last night after the party? She wound her way over to the Keurig, popped in an espresso pod and pressed the button. Caffeine in hand, she joined Jake at the island and pulled out a stool. "You seem preoccupied. Or are you deliberately ignoring me?"

He threw her an irritated look. "Do you blame me?"

Haley blinked, taken aback by his disgruntled tone. "What? You're looking at me like I did something."

He set down his iPad and frowned at her. "You really don't remember, do you?"

Haley's stomach tightened. She was reluctant to admit that she couldn't recall anything about how the evening had ended. "Remember what? I remember the party. We invited the neighbors over for drinks and desserts. Did something happen I don't know about?" She had a feeling Jake was about to tell her, and that she wasn't going to like what he had to say.

He tightened his lips before answering. "You made a complete fool of yourself in front of our neighbors. You got so drunk I had to take you upstairs and put you to bed."

Haley's mouth fell open. "Don't be ridiculous. I've never been drunk in my life. I only had a glass-and-a-half of wine."

Jake shook his head in disbelief. "You must have been partaking more freely than that. Maybe you were trying to calm your nerves or something, but you got so tipsy you were falling over people."

Haley sat in shocked silence as she tried to digest what he was saying. Had she got drunk? She did remember the wine going to her head more quickly than usual. If she'd actually got so drunk that she was falling over people, no wonder Jake was upset. He was so straight-laced, so black-and-white —he would hate that she'd made a fool of herself the very first time they'd invited their neighbors over.

"The thing is, Jake," she said hesitantly. "I didn't drink much at all. I never have more than a glass or two when I'm hosting. It's too hard to stay on top of things."

Jake let out an exasperated sigh. "Well, that's not what happened last night. Ask any of the neighbors. I was the one stuck apologizing to everyone. You ruined the whole party. After I came back downstairs, they all made their excuses and left."

Haley stared into her coffee cup pressing hard for any shred of a memory of Jake accompanying her upstairs, but her mind was blank. None of it made sense. Why would she all of a sudden start drinking so heavily that she passed out? It wasn't like her at all. She'd made one terrible mistake in her life, and the idea of getting drunk enough to make another was abhorrent to her.

And then a frightening thought occurred to her. Her gut tightened, and when she spoke her voice shook. "I think I know what happened, Jake. One of the neighbors must have slipped something into my drink. It proves what I suspected all along. One of them is behind this attempt to sabotage me. I don't know why, maybe they're getting some kind of sadistic kick out of it."

Jake leaned back against the bar stool and pressed his fingers to his temples. "Haley, please stop! I'm begging you. Our neighbors are a bunch of decent, hard-working people like ourselves. They're not creeps. You saw that for yourself last night. And Edith and Harold are elderly recluses who never leave their house. I can guarantee everyone has better things to do than to sneak into our house and throw out our pots while we're at work, and they certainly aren't going around drugging people."

"Why won't you listen to me?" Haley demanded. "It's the only explanation for what happened. I started feeling dizzy and disoriented almost at once, I'd barely drunk a few sips. My glass was sitting beside the platters of desserts when I went to the front door to look for Edith and Harold. Anyone could have slipped something into it."

Jake stood abruptly. "I've had enough. This is getting completely out of hand. Just because a couple of nasty things happened to you in the past, it doesn't mean our neighbors are drugging you."

"You don't know that! You scarcely know them."

"Maybe I don't know you all that well either," Jake retorted, his eyes glinting with anger. "Because I'm beginning to think you're paranoid about everyone."

Before Haley had a chance to respond, he strode out of the kitchen, down the hall, and slammed the front door behind him. Moments later, she heard the sound of his car starting up and pulling out of the cul-de-sac. She dropped her head into her hands. Her world felt like it was crashing down around her. She'd dared to believe things would improve once she and Jake were married and he was living in the house with her—that he would take her side and help her get to the bottom of things. But he didn't believe her. He thought she was going crazy.

Haley let out a heavy sigh and laid her head down on her arms. Maybe she was losing it. Maybe there was something medically wrong with her. If she'd blacked out last night, perhaps she'd blacked out on other occasions too and didn't even know it.

After a few minutes, she sat up and sipped her coffee, reflecting on the growing number of inexplicable episodes in her life. Aside from the possibility that she'd accidentally thrown the wok out herself, she definitely hadn't sent that awful email to her boss, or damaged her own car, or written a note telling herself to die. The things that were happening to her were making her paranoid. She got to her feet, walked over to the kitchen drawer and pulled out a composition notebook. One-by-one, she jotted down the incidents in an approximate time line as best she could remember. If Jake didn't believe her theory that someone was messing with her, she would have to figure things out for herself.

She couldn't ask the police to find out who was stalking her. They might start digging into her past and uncover things she didn't want anyone to know about. Her thoughts drifted back to the awful thing she'd done. The last thing she needed now was cops asking about the newspaper articles with Emma Murray's face plastered all over them.

ELEVEN YEARS EARLIER

"Who's the new chick?" Lachlan jerked her pert chin at the petite blonde who had slipped quietly into a seat in the back row of their honors biology class. The girl sat, unmoving, shoulders hunched, eyes firmly fixed on her desk.

"Only a loser changes schools halfway through sophomore year," Tina hissed.

"No idea who she is," Vivian said, a sinister grin forming on her heavily outlined lips. "But we should make it our mission to find out."

"Yeah," Lachlan drawled, fluffing out her mane of black waves. "Let's *befriend* the poor lost lamb. She looks like she needs our help."

They dissolved into a fit of laughter, the underlying intent all too clear.

While the others were busy touching up their make up in their iPhone cameras, Haley cast a curious glance at the newcomer. For a brief moment, the girl met her gaze, giving her a tentative smile. Haley fought the temptation to smile back, instead tossing her head as she turned back to her quad sisters. "Can you believe that freak just smiled at me? One of those lip-trembling, please-be-my-friend-because-I'm-so-lonely smiles."

Lachlan let out a contemptuous snort. "I've got this one. Watch and learn."

She got to her feet and minced to the back of the class-room, swinging her hips as several of the guys ogled her long, lean figure.

The other quads watched as Lachlan bent over the new girl's desk, affording everyone in the vicinity an indulgent display of her cleavage. She exchanged a few words with the stranger before strutting back to her desk, her lips curved into a snide smile.

"Well?" Tina demanded. "What's the scoop?"

"Ugh, *bor-ing* beyond belief." Lachlan swatted her hand through the air. "Her name's Emma. Her dad got transferred here with the bank he works at. She's gonna be way too easy. I invited her to sit with us at lunch."

And so it began. For the next few weeks, the quads hung around Emma until they'd gleaned enough information to start making her life miserable. Her homework mysteriously disappeared, vulgar graffiti defaced her locker, somehow gum found its way into her hair and mushed French fries into her backpack. A photoshopped picture of her with an elongated jaw and prominent ears was submitted to the year-book. One of the guys at the quad squad's beck and call feigned interest in her and then posted the pathetic texts she sent him on social media. For weeks on end, a host of increasingly malicious diversions kept the quads and their groupies amused. All the while, Emma believed her new friends were helping her through a trying semester at a new school.

The day Haley got a hold of Emma's diary elevated her rank among her quad sisters for a few brief hours. But what she chose to do with it next was what ripped them apart forever.

Lachlan was the first to pass her driving test, and her wealthy parents rewarded her with a brand-new, white Prius. Unbeknownst to them, she regularly drove her quad sisters all over town in it. The day it all went down, they'd gone to a local coffee shop after school for mochas and taken Emma along for sport. Tina had purchased a powder laxative and added it to her drink. Afterward, Lachlan offered to give them all a ride home. Emma, who lived close to the coffee shop, was already feeling queasy and insisted on walking. The others piled back into the Prius, snickering and nudging each other as Emma tripped her way down the street, clutching her stomach. That's when Haley discovered Emma had left her backpack in the car.

"No way!" Haley said in a breathless whisper, undoing the buckles and getting ready to rummage around inside. "This is perfect. The freak forgot her backpack."

"Score! This oughta be good." Vivian gave Tina a high five. "What you got, Hales?"

"One classwork binder." Haley tossed it to the floor and yanked out a composition notebook next. "Biology home-work. We could for sure do something with that. And here's her volleyball shirt—that's definitely going missing." She fished around inside the backpack some more and pulled out a notebook with a tiny gold lock. "Check this out! I think I just hit the jackpot." She held the book aloft for the others to see. "It's a diary."

"What? Give it here!" Vivian yelled from the passenger seat, trying to snatch it out of Haley's fingers and bumping the steering wheel in the process.

"Hey! Knock it off!" Lachlan cried. "You're gonna make me crash. My parents will kill me if I get in a wreck with you lot in the car."

"Let me see that!" Tina held out her hand for the diary.

"Nuh-uh." Haley slipped it between her thigh and the side of the car. "I found it. I get to look inside first." She reached for the backpack again and began searching through the smaller pockets for the key to open the lock.

Tina frowned at her. "What are you doing?"

"Looking for the key."

"You don't need one," Tina snapped back. "Give it here. I'll show you how to open it."

"I got this!" Haley's fingers closed around a pair of scissors in Emma's pencil case. The diary was too big a triumph for her to relinquish to any of the other girls. She pulled out the scissors with a flourish and jammed them into the tiny padlock on the diary, forcing it open. "And, we're in!" she announced triumphantly.

As she flicked through pages of doodles and entries, she began reading out loud Emma's most intimate confessions, everything from what she hated about herself, to her thoughts on saving whales and the environment. Within minutes, the girls were busting their sides, cackling sacrilegiously at each new reveal.

"She's … even … lamer than I thought," Vivian rasped, scarcely able to stop laughing long enough to get the words out. "I can't … believe … the stuff she writes."

"Hey, listen to this!" Haley lowered her voice to an awed whisper. "Sounds like Emma's got the hots for Mr. Davidson."

"Our *English* teacher?" Tina crumpled her forehead in disbelief. "Are you serious?"

"Oh yeah." Haley swiftly scanned the page in front of her. "She's into him in a big way."

"You've got to be kidding me!" Lachlan exclaimed. "He's at least thirty-five."

Tina tried to snatch the diary out of Haley's hands again. "So what does she have to say about him?"

"Shut up and listen." Vivian narrowed her eyes at Tina. "Read it to us, Hales."

Haley began reading in an exaggerated, breathless tone. "To my one, true, love, Erik Davidson. The sound of your voice washes over me each morning like a soft rain. Every time I hear you speak, it's as though you're speaking only to me. Your soft lips press against mine, the fire of your passion shooting through me like a comet—" Haley stopped reading abruptly and looked around at the other girls wide-eyed. "This is pure gold. We've got to do something with this."

"You *think*?" Tina said. "We need to get Davidson's eyeballs on it for starters."

Vivian arched a heavily powdered brow at Haley. "This one's on you. You found it, it's your job to make sure this drivel finds its way to Davidson's desk."

For a brief moment, Haley hesitated, considering the repercussions. But they paled in comparison to the adulation that would come her way from her quad sisters, if she left the diary on Mr. Davidson's desk. Ignoring the voice in her head that cautioned against such a deep betrayal of Emma's trust, Haley grinned around at the other girls as she ripped the page from the diary in one decisive tug. "I've got a better idea. I'm gonna pin it to the noticeboard outside Davidson's classroom and let the whole school gawk at it."

"Love it! Love it! *Love* it!" Lachlan sang, her tempo rising with each pronouncement as she slapped the steering wheel.

"Let's do it right now," Tina said. "We need to dump Emma's backpack off at the school anyway. We'll tell her she forgot it at school, that way anyone could have taken the page from her diary."

The plan took shape as the girls drove back to school, riding on a wave of euphoria at the thought of the humiliation about to descend once the lovestruck Emma's diary page was discovered and distributed.

Back at the school, the corridors were close to deserted, only the occasional student or teacher passing along them. Lachlan wasted no time emptying out Emma's backpack next to the lockers and then tossing it to one side before they made their way to Mr. Davidson's classroom. Haley scanned up and down the corridor in both directions before pinning the incriminating page to the English department notice-board. Above it, she placed a Post-it note with the words: *Guess who Mr. Davidson's secret lover is?*

When she was done, the quads headed out to the parking lot, giggling hysterically in anticipation of what the next day's big reveal would bring. Haley spent the remainder of the evening in her room exulting in her infamy—she might have been the last to join the quads, but she was no longer their most insignificant member.

The fallout was instantaneous. The handwritten diary page was discovered before first period began the following day, and within minutes, kids were messaging pictures of it to each other, taking bets on who Mr. Davidson's secret lover was. Haley was on a high the entire first period, but by second period, things had taken a turn she didn't anticipate. The police arrived on campus. Mr. Davidson didn't show up for the rest of his classes. And the rumor mill was just getting started.

"Did you know he's a child molester?"

"He's been having affairs with students for years."

"The police think he might be part of a sex-trafficking ring."

"He seduces girls and films them."

By late afternoon, the handwriting on the diary page had been identified as Emma Murray's. When she was called out of math class, the quad sisters exchanged satisfied grins. A thoroughly humiliated Emma would be forced to admit that it was all fantasy on her part, and Mr. Davidson would return to work, exonerated of any wrongdoing. It would all blow over by day's end.

For the remainder of the day, Haley reigned supreme as queen of the quads. Lachlan, Tina, and Vivian even took her out for a shake after school to congratulate her on the feat she'd pulled off. Little did Haley know that night was the last night she would sleep well for years to come.

The next morning, the campus was swarming with law enforcement, and the interrogations began in earnest. The cops talked to everyone in Emma's classes, paying special attention to her "friends." The quad squad was separated and interviewed. Each question churned up more fear and dread in Haley's heart.

"Did Emma have any enemies?"

"What about a boyfriend, or an ex-boyfriend?"

"Did you know she had a crush on Mr. Davidson?"

"Did you ever see Emma and Mr. Davidson together?"

"Did Emma ever hint that Mr. Davidson touched her inappropriately?"

The relentless questioning went on for days until the police finally closed the case. There simply wasn't enough evidence to prosecute Mr. Davidson for having sex with a minor, but the very hint of scandal had been enough to force him to resign from his position.

Emma Murray could do nothing to absolve him—she'd hanged herself the night her diary went public.

12

---

*S*ix months to the day when her car was vandalized, Haley received a gift basket from The Fruit Gourmet. She knew the exact date it was delivered because she'd begun documenting everything in her notebook—not just the harassment and the disturbing things that were happening to her, but also every occasion when she sensed someone was watching her. She made a careful note of when and where each incident happened, who she suspected, and why. If she was ever forced to go to the police, at least she'd have a detailed log of events and suspects to show them. She grimaced as she reviewed her notes. As disheartening a thought as it was, if it turned out she was losing her mind, then her notes might even prove useful to whichever psychologist she ended up seeing. She'd already succumbed to taking extra strength sleeping pills in an effort to curb the insomnia, maybe something to tackle her paranoia next was in order.

The day the basket was delivered, she'd arrived home from work ahead of Jake. He'd been working late more often than not in the weeks since they'd hosted the disastrous neighborhood gathering. She still couldn't entirely shake her suspicion that someone had tampered with her drink that night, but Jake remained convinced that she'd simply made a fool of herself by drinking too much. Haley could feel a distance growing between them, and it broke her heart, but she wasn't sure what to do about it. It was hard to feel close to your spouse when he dismissed your fears and thought you were crazy—not that she could blame him. Some days she wondered as much herself.

She'd been going out of her way to avoid her neighbors, checking to make sure no one was in their driveway before exiting her house. To her dismay, Jake had struck up quite the friendship with the men who lived in the cul-de-sac following their party. She couldn't help wondering what he'd told them about that night. That his wife was losing it? That she was an alcoholic? Popping pills like candy?

Haley pulled into her driveway after work and, after throwing a quick glance in her rearview mirror to make sure no one was around, climbed out of her car and locked it—checking it twice as she was now in the habit of doing. She walked up to her front door, observing without moving her head, her neighbor, Edith, taking a quick peek from behind the safety of her curtain. Haley had grown used to her curious next-door neighbors' ways—in an odd way it was comforting to know they kept a close eye on things. Ironically, it was also the only way anyone would ever know if anything happened to them. The day the curtain failed to twitch would be the day Haley would call the authorities to conduct a welfare check.

She stooped down to pick up a couple of parcels on her front doorstep: a small bubble-wrap package from Amazon for Jake, and a large box from The Fruit Gourmet addressed to her. She frowned, wracking her brain as to who it could be from. Nick, perhaps—thanking her for a job well done on their last case? He'd gifted her a bottle of champagne as a thank you in the past, but he always left it on her desk in the office. Still, he knew where she lived—it was possible he'd had it sent directly to her home. Inside the kitchen, Haley set the parcels on the counter and tossed her keys and purse down next to them. After grabbing a bottle of water from the refrigerator, she sat down at the kitchen island to open the box from The Fruit Gourmet. Someone knew she had a penchant for fruit.

She sliced open the packing tape, and opened up the cardboard box to reveal a royal blue gift box with an embossed company emblem on the front. She sniffed at it tentatively. Something didn't smell all that great. Gingerly, she lifted out the gift box and pulled off the lid, immediately reeling back from the odor that assailed her nostrils. Black flecks flitted past her eyes as tiny fruit flies zipped away from the fermenting mush in the box. Stomach roiling, she hurriedly slammed the lid back on and raced out to the garbage can at the back of the house. She tossed the entire box inside, almost gagging in the process before returning to the kitchen. The odor of rotten fruit lingered in the air as she threw open the window, staring in dismay at the fruit flies flitting around inside her house. She quickly filled a couple of glass dishes with apple cider and added a drop of dish soap to each one before covering them with plastic wrap and poking holes in the top to serve as traps. Hopefully they would serve their purpose before Jake came home. He would be disgusted by the invasion—his obsession with cleanliness made him particularly averse to insects or animals in the house.

She turned her attention to the cardboard shipping box the tray of fruit had been nestled in. Poking out from the peanuts that filled it, she spotted a small, white envelope. She reached for it and tore it open, staring in horror at the single word printed on the card inside.

Rot!

The card fluttered to the ground. Haley staggered backward, one hand to her chest. Her sudden struggle to breathe had nothing to do with the rotten smell, and everything to do with the suffocating fear rising up inside her. What sick and twisted person had sent this? Why were they tormenting her like this? After gulping a calming breath, she took a hesitant step toward the box and examined the label more closely. It wasn't a proper shipping label at all. It had been printed out on a laser computer, but it was evident someone had hand-delivered the box to the front door. Her heart slugged against her chest, panic descending. In the midst of her confusion, another thought occurred to her. Her nosy neighbor, Edith, might have seen who had delivered it.

Without taking a moment to second-guess herself, Haley dashed out of her house and ran next door intent on banging on the door until Edith answered it. This time, Haley wouldn't let her go until she gave her the information she needed.

After a third round of hammering on the door, interspersed by several frantic rings of the doorbell, Haley finally heard the sound of shuffling on the other side, and then the door opened the customary few inches. As soon as Edith's face appeared in the crack, the words began spilling from Haley's lips. "Please can I come in? Something's happened and I really need your help."

The old woman's rheumy eyes filled with alarm behind her glasses. Her puckered lips parted and snapped together once and then, to Haley's surprise, she unlatched the door and pulled it open. For a moment, Haley stood stunned on the doorstep. She wasn't sure if she was more shocked at the fact that Edith had opened the door to her, or at the sight of all the stuff that was piled high behind her, spanning the entire length of the hallway. No wonder Edith and Harold never came out of their house. They were big time hoarders —or at least one of them was, and the other one put up with it. Haley took a quick breath of stale air infused with decay and age, resigning herself to the fact that her neighbor's house would probably stink almost as bad as the rotten fruit fermenting in her garbage can. Unwilling to let the opportunity go by to grill Edith, she willed herself to step over the threshold and into a mausoleum of moldering stuff.

Edith turned and began shuffling down the narrow strip of dark hallway. Unbidden, Haley followed her. There was nowhere else to go. Walls of boxes, tubs and papers closed off any alternative routes.

When they reached the kitchen, Haley swallowed back her dismay at the dismal state of the room. It too was stacked high with broken appliances, empty boxes, congealed food and dirty dishes. A table was jammed against one wall, two chairs pushed beneath it. Edith sat down and gestured to Haley to do the same. She tried not to grimace as she pulled out a rickety wooden chair with a stained fabric seat. She could handle the mess for a few minutes to get the information she needed. She just hoped Edith didn't offer her a cup of tea or coffee. Instead, the old woman interlaced her fingers on the table in front of her and blinked expectantly at Haley.

"The thing is, someone's been harassing me," Haley blurted out. "It's been going on for quite some time. Today, they left a box of rotten fruit on my front doorstep. A couple of months ago they left a threatening note under my windshield wiper. They've damaged my car before, and I think they watch me at times." Haley hesitated, searching for the right words. "I know you and Harold keep a close eye on everyone who comes and goes in the cul-de-sac. Did you happen to see anyone at my front door today, or any strangers hanging around the neighborhood?" Haley sucked in her breath and waited for Edith's response.

Heavy footsteps filled the silence. The hairs on the back of Haley's neck rose. Slowly, she turned her head and peered over her shoulder. Her pulse ratcheted up. A balding, round-faced man with reddened, piggish eyes huddled together in displeasure stood in the doorway. *Harold!* He pulled out a crumpled tissue and wiped a drip from his bulbous nose. His belly jiggled beneath his thin cotton shirt as he took a step toward them. "What's going on here, Edith?" His voice was low and raspy, his teeth yellow and uneven behind thin lips. Haley could tell by Edith's hunched posture that Harold was the one who controlled everything that went on in this house, including who was admitted. She'd put Edith in a bad situation by inviting herself in. She needed to do something to make it right.

Getting to her feet, she extended a hand. "You must be Harold."

He stood there, punching his fist repeatedly into the palm of his hand. "Who's asking?" His voice was sharper now, commanding, his eyes flicking to Edith.

She seemed to have shrunk into an even smaller space than her tiny five-foot frame comprised. "This is Haley Wilder, our next-door neighbor," she explained in a birdlike whisper. "She needs my help with something."

Harold's eyes flickered with rage. "Help? You're in no position to help anyone. What good are you?"

Haley rocked back on her heels, shocked at the disparaging tone Harold was taking with his sister. She threw a quick glance at Edith, but it was obvious the woman was conditioned to his abuse and not about to stand up to him.

"As a matter of fact, Edith's been extremely helpful," Haley retorted.

Harold's eyes lingered on her for a moment. "You're not welcome here. Get on back to your own property. If I catch you here again, I'll call the police." He edged closer, his eyes boring into her. "And I don't think you'd like them stopping by, would you?"

Haley's heart jolted in her chest, the loaded statement slamming into her like a punch to the gut. Did Harold know something, or was she reading too much into his threat? Maybe he'd done some research on her and found out what had happened in her past. After all, he and Edith were an inquisitive pair.

"Get her out of here," Harold ordered his sister, before slumping down in the chair Haley had vacated.

Obediently, Edith got to her feet and led the way out of the kitchen and back down the strip of hallway.

"You don't have to let him speak to you like that, you know," Haley whispered.

Edith blinked blankly at her from behind her thick glasses, and then turned to open the door. As Haley stepped toward it, Edith muttered, "I saw who dropped off your parcel."

Haley cast a quick glance over her shoulder to make sure Harold wasn't watching them. "Who?"

"It was a man—around three this afternoon." She hesitated, frowning. "About your husband's size and height. In fact, he looked a bit like him."

13

---

*H*aley's mouth fell open. She stared at Edith for a long moment, and then shook her head. "You must be mistaken. My husband was at work all day. He's not home yet."

"Well, I didn't get a good look, so I can't say for sure," Edith said, pulling nervously at her ear. "He was only there for a few seconds."

"It might have looked like him at a quick glance," Haley said, softening her tone. "How well can you see my front door from behind your curtain anyway?" She gestured to the family room. "May I?"

Edith peered down the hallway and then gave a tentative nod.

Haley squeezed through a narrow opening in the wall of boxes fencing off the family room and pulled aside the fraying curtain. She had a reasonably good view of her front door from there, but the window was filthy and, if she had to guess by the way Edith had squinted at her through her glasses when she opened the door, she likely hadn't had her eyes checked in years. Haley sighed inwardly as she pulled the curtain back into place. Edith couldn't be relied on to identify who had dropped off the package. The only thing she could count on with any certainty was that it was a man —that much Edith would have been able to make out from here.

"Edith! What are you doing?" Harold roared from the kitchen.

The old woman's fingers twitched and she scratched at her cheek distractedly as she shot a pleading look at Haley.

"I'm leaving," Haley assured her. "If you ever need help—" Her voice trailed off. No sense in beating around the bush. She needed to speak plainly if she was to be of any assistance. Lowering her voice to a whisper, she added, "If you want to leave him, I'll help you find somewhere else to live. You don't have to put up with that kind of abuse." With a final wave, she exited through the front door, Edith immediately pushing it closed behind her. Haley couldn't help but wonder if she would ever see the inside of the house again. It broke her heart to think that Edith was living out her days with such a monster. Maybe Harold owned the house and she was financially dependent on him. Haley frowned to herself as she walked back up the path to her own front door. She would give the director of Big Brothers Big Sisters a call as soon as she got a chance. He would know what services were available to help Edith get away from that brute of a brother of hers.

Was it possible Harold was behind what was happening? The thought chilled her. He'd been furious when he'd found her in his house. And Edith was obviously terrified of him, she might have been trying to cover for him by saying she'd seen a man who looked like Jake drop off the fruit basket. The only question was why—as far as Haley knew Harold didn't have any apparent motive to harass her.

Back inside her house, she made herself a cup of peppermint tea, musing over Edith's bombshell. Deep down, Haley had a hard time believing that Edith had seen someone who looked like Jake dropping off the parcel, but she had to be sure. She wouldn't be able to sleep tonight if she had even a smidgeon of doubt. The truth was that everything unsettling had started happening around the time she met Jake. Haley set down her cup with a heavy sigh. She had to get rid of this insidious seed of doubt about her own husband that Edith had planted in her mind. Reaching for her purse, she pulled out her phone and dialed Jake's office. He would hate it if he knew she was checking up on him, but with a bit of luck he would never find out.

"Axis Financial Services, Rochelle speaking."

Haley's heart raced. She hadn't taken the time to think through exactly how she was going to extract the information she needed. "Hi, Rochelle, it's Haley Wilder."

"Oh hi, Haley, do you want me to put you through to Jake?"

"No, it's fine, thanks." She let out an apologetic laugh. "Actually, I was hoping to ask you something, woman-to-woman."

There was a long pause on the other end of the line, and then Rochelle said hesitantly, "Uh, sure. What's up?"

"It's a little embarrassing, to be honest," Haley continued, feigning a chagrined tone, "but one of my co-workers thought she saw my husband in a cafe with another woman this afternoon. I don't know if she's just trying to stir up trouble for me, or if I have something to be worried about. Do you … happen to know if Jake was at the office all afternoon?"

"He sure was," Rochelle replied, sounding relieved to be the bearer of good news. "We had a quarterly department meeting today. I ordered in lunch for everyone. No one's been out of the office." She hesitated and then added, "That colleague of yours is either mistaken, or trying to do your head in."

Haley let out an exaggerated sigh of relief. "Thank you, Rochelle. I thought as much, but she was so insistent it was him that she put a seed of suspicion in my head. Promise me you won't mention this to Jake. I feel stupid for doubting him. Newlywed jitters, I guess."

"Don't worry, my lips are sealed," Rochelle said breezily. "I'm glad I could put your mind at ease."

"Thanks again," Haley said, ending the call. She set her phone down on the counter and sank back in her bar stool. As she'd suspected, Edith had been mistaken.

She scrunched her eyes closed and waited until the knot in her chest unwound. It bothered her that lying still came so easily to her, even all these years later. She'd lied proficiently to the police when they'd asked her about Emma's diary. She'd been so smooth that they'd swallowed every word she'd fed them. But then lying was one of the things the quad squad had excelled at. Haley twisted her fingers together. Now that she'd done it, she felt bad for deceiving Rochelle and quizzing her about Jake's whereabouts. Maybe she didn't deserve a good man like Jake. It would serve her right if her relationship fell apart thanks to her paranoia, and if it continued along the path it was on, it might very well do just that.

Haley stood and paced across the kitchen. Now that she'd eliminated Jake as a suspect, she went back to her theory that Edith was covering for Harold. If he was her stalker, it was time Haley did something to protect herself. Harold was a scary character—the type of man who could erupt in fury at the slightest provocation. The first thing she needed to do was install a high-tech camera security system —the alarm system they had wouldn't suffice. The second thing she intended to do was get a dog. Jake wouldn't be too happy about it, clean freak that he was, but it was her house after all. A guard dog could warn her if someone was prowling around outside, or messing with her car. Her mind made up, she reached for her laptop and began browsing dog breeds and nearby kennels in earnest. By the time Jake arrived home from work, she'd already called a breeder with a litter of German shepherds for sale and made an appointment to visit them the following day after work.

Jake eyed her warily as though he sensed something had happened. "How was your day?" he ventured.

Haley grimaced. "All right, until I got home."

He frowned, swatting at a fruit fly, his gaze traveling around the room searching for its source.

"I can tell you where that fly came from," Haley said. "Someone sent me a box of rotten fruit today. I tossed it in the outdoor trash."

Jake blinked, digesting her words as he swatted at another fly. "Yikes! Well that explains the bugs in here. I've never heard of an expired fruit delivery before. I'm sure the company will replace it."

"That's not the point. It wasn't a gift from a satisfied customer," Haley explained, trying to curb the irritation in her voice. She picked up the note card and held it out to Jake.

He took it from her and studied it for a long moment.

"It's still happening," Haley said with a tremor.

Jake pulled out a stool and sat down beside her, a chastened expression on his face. "I guess you were right after all. I'm sorry, sweetheart."

Heartened by his response, Haley turned the laptop screen around to face him. "I think it's time I got a dog for protection. I'm scared to be home when you're not here. And even when you are, anyone could be sneaking around outside without either of us knowing. We need a better security system too. I want to install cameras around the perimeter of the house."

Jake blew out a breath and leaned back in his chair. "Cameras are one thing, but a German shepherd pup is a lot of work, Hales. You know I don't like dogs to begin with. And we're gone all day. A dog is gonna go bonkers by itself. It will chew everything in sight. Besides, they shed a lot. You know how I am about keeping things clean. We'd have to vacuum this place every day."

"I don't care about the extra work. It would be worth it to make me feel safe," Haley countered. "There's a sicko out there bent on harassing me, and I don't know how far he's going to take it. I know you didn't really believe it at first, but you can't deny it anymore." Haley gestured at the card. "This isn't the behavior of a sane individual. One of these days he might try and harm me physically."

Her voice broke and Jake reached for her and gathered her in his arms. She pressed her head against his chest and began to sob quietly. "I'm so scared, Jake. I even went next door to ask Edith if she saw who delivered the parcel."

"What did she say?" he asked in a measured tone.

"She ... didn't see anyone," Haley answered, the lie falling effortlessly from her lips. She couldn't risk Jake marching over there and confronting Edith. The poor woman was frazzled enough already. "Her brother was there. He's a nasty character. He ran me out of their house. I'm half-afraid it might be him who's behind all this."

"He's just a grumpy old man," Jake soothed. "Anthony and Stan told me all about him. He's been that way for years, never leaves the house. But, if it makes you feel any better, we'll get a dog. So long as it's trained properly. I don't want to be stuck cleaning up after it."

"Thanks, babe." Haley swallowed back a sob. "Don't worry, I won't dump the responsibility for it on you. I can take it to weekend training courses, and I'll hire someone to come by during the day while we're at work to take it for walks. We won't let it go upstairs or lay on the couches so you don't need to worry about dog hair—"

"We'll figure it out," Jake said, giving her a reassuring squeeze. "The most important thing is that you feel safe."

Haley wiped the tears from her eyes. "I've made an appointment to look at some pups tomorrow. Will you come with me?" She held her breath, waiting for his response, needing him to be on her side, but not wanting to pressure him. She desperately wanted them to stop drifting any farther apart and to be on the same page about things going forward.

"Sure," Jake said after a long pause. "Let's go pick you out a guard dog."

Haley threw him a grateful smile and kissed him on the cheek. He may have had his doubts about some of the things that had happened to her, but the rotten fruit delivery proved she wasn't losing her mind. Whoever was waging a vendetta against her had struck again. Lance's ominous warning had been right all along—someone had it in for her.

*T*hree weeks later, they brought home a female German shepherd pup that Haley named Katniss. As she'd promised, Haley took the pup to weekend training classes religiously, and even hired a local dog walker to come by during the week to exercise Katniss while she and Jake were at work. Their next-door neighbor, Jim Markham, had been kind enough to install the heavy-duty doggie door Haley ordered from Amazon. She'd asked Jake to tackle the project first—still horribly embarrassed by what had happened at the neighborhood gathering they'd hosted—but Jake wasn't particularly handy, and he'd wanted the job done right.

"I need to apologize for my behavior when you came over for our little get together," Haley said to Jim, as he finished screwing the door in place. "That wasn't typical of me at all. I didn't even get to say goodnight to anyone."

Jim waved aside her apology with a broad smile. "No worries. I'm glad it wasn't a seizure or something—you passed out cold, it happened so quickly it spooked everyone."

Haley rumpled her brow. "It was odd, I felt like I was

drugged or something. You didn't ... notice anyone touch my glass, by chance?"

Jim sat up straighter, clutching his screw gun. His expression darkened. "Are you suggesting one of us spiked your drink?"

"No! No, of course not," Haley said, flustered. "I ... just wish I knew what happened."

Jim got to his feet and brushed off his work pants. He gave her an awkward grin. "It's okay, your husband explained about the sleeping pills."

Haley stared at him in shock, opening her mouth to respond and then deciding against it until she'd had a word with Jake first. No wonder no one had mentioned the incident since—they all thought she'd been high. But nothing could be further from the truth.

"Katniss should be all set now to go in and out whenever she wants," Jim said, demonstrating the swing door.

"Thank you ... again," Haley stammered, as she saw him out. Confusion balled in her stomach as she reflected on what he'd told her. She'd only started taking the sleeping pills after the party. Why had Jake lied about it? Her face burned with shame as the realization hit her. Her husband must have been so mortified by her behavior that night that he'd made up a cover story to tell the neighbors.

DESPITE HALEY'S BEST EFFORTS, Katniss soon became a bone of contention between her and Jake. The pup was naturally curious and forever getting into things, chewing up stuff they left out while they were at work, and having accidents that had to be cleaned up when they arrived home. To make matters worse, Jake complained incessantly about the dog hair even though Haley followed through on her commitment to vacuum daily.

Things escalated until one morning Haley walked into the family room and caught Jake swinging a kick at Katniss to get her off the couch.

"Jake!" she cried, rushing over to grab the pup. "What do you think you're doing?"

He turned and glared at her. "We had an agreement, remember? The dog's not allowed on the couch. She's supposed to stay in her bed on the floor."

"That's no reason to kick her. She's not doing any harm. Besides, it's not as if you're allergic or anything," Haley pointed out.

"That's irrelevant. I don't want to get up from the couch and find dog hair all over my clothes," Jake snapped back. "Is that too much to ask?"

"Of course not, I'm training her not to jump up on the furniture," Haley said, rubbing Katniss's neck while avoiding meeting Jake's accusatory gaze. Truth be told, she had been kind of lax about letting the pup on the couch when Jake wasn't around. She felt safe curled up with Katniss on her lap.

"Clearly the training's not working. And she's a destroyer. We need to get rid of her."

Haley threw her husband a horrified look. "Don't be ridiculous! She only chews things she thinks we left out for her to play with. Remember why we got her in the first place. Someone's stalking me, Jake. We need a dog for protection. You agreed to this."

He let out a weary sigh, rubbing a hand across the back of his neck. "You're right. Your safety comes first. I'll try and be more patient if you promise to keep her off the couch." He walked over to the door. "I gotta go to work. See you later."

Haley nodded, only partly mollified. Although she'd hidden her outrage, she'd been shocked to see a cruel streak in Jake for the first time. Maybe she was pushing it by asking him to live with a large German shepherd when he wasn't a dog person to begin with. Katniss didn't seem to be warming up to him either, and now Haley knew why. This mightn't have been the first time he'd swung a mean-spirited kick at her.

She closed Katniss in the kitchen, grabbed her purse and keys, and made her way out to her car. Apart from the upheaval Katniss had caused, the past few weeks had been relatively uneventful as far as stalking incidents went. The new cameras they'd installed on the perimeter of the house to record anyone wandering around, or approaching the front door, gave Haley some peace of mind that her stalker could no longer loiter freely outside. She climbed into her car, reversed down the driveway and pulled out of the cul-de-sac, her thoughts immediately zeroing in on the day's work ahead of her.

All in all, things weren't going too badly at Huntington and Dodd—she loved her new job, and she and Natalie had become close friends over the past few months. Haley was even beginning to warm up to Lance. After engaging him in conversation on a couple of occasions, she'd discovered that he lived with his elderly mother and devoted all his free time to looking after her. It seemed Natalie was right after all—Lance was a little eccentric but perfectly harmless and an all-around good sort.

Haley merged onto the freeway heading downtown in the direction of the office, her mind already preoccupied by the workload waiting for her. So far, she'd managed to hold things together and keep Nick satisfied, despite her many sleepless nights and the brain fog that dogged her, but it was taking its toll. She was exhausted most of the time, and Natalie wasn't the only one at the office who had commented on the dark blotches beneath Haley's eyes.

Spotting her exit up ahead, she turned on her blinker and

moved into the right lane. Braking as she exited the freeway, her brain belatedly registered something was amiss. She pumped the brakes furiously, but, to her horror, the car didn't slow down. Her muscles locked as she slammed the brake to the floorboard and held it there. Seconds later the crunching sound of metal filled the air as she plowed into the Toyota Tundra in front of her. Her airbag deployed, instantly pinning her to the seat, obscuring her view as an acrid smell filled her nostrils. She sat there stunned, vaguely registering the fact that an airbag wasn't a big, soft, fluffy pillow at all—it felt as if someone had whacked her in the chest with a two by four.

Within seconds, some good Samaritan wrenched open her car door and yelled, "Are you all right?"

Haley blinked, her view of the stranger blocked by the airbag. Had she really rear-ended a truck on her way to work? "I ... my chest hurts." She fumbled for her seatbelt, but it was locked in place like a vice.

"Everything's gonna be fine," the stranger soothed. "Don't move. The ambulance is on its way."

Haley tried to nod, but her neck hurt. She was too parched to talk—the stench of the ruptured airbag had left a burning sensation in her throat. How had this happened? Did she wait too long to deploy the brakes? She must have been distracted—worrying about the projects for Nick she was dangerously close to falling behind on.

She closed her eyes, but the stranger's panicked voice jolted her back to the moment. "Ma'am, can you hear me? You need to stay awake! The ambulance will be here any minute. What's your name?"

"Haley," she rasped. "Haley Wilder. What about the people in the truck? Are they okay?"

"Everyone's fine. Just a little whiplash," her good Samaritan replied.

The wail of sirens soon filled the air. Within minutes, the police were directing traffic around her and paramedics flocked to her aid, peppering her with questions.

"Can you feel your legs?"

"Where does it hurt?"

"Do you have any medical conditions?"

Somewhere in the middle of the chaos, a policeman took a brief statement.

Half-dazed, Haley wheezed out the appropriate responses. Before she realized what was happening, the paramedics had extricated her from her seat and loaded her onto a stretcher trolley.

"Can you grab my purse?" she asked weakly. "It's on the passenger seat."

One of the paramedics reached inside and slid it out.

"What about my car?" Haley asked.

"The police will have it towed for you. Is there someone you want them to call?"

"My husband, Jake Wilder." She recited his number for the paramedic, barely able to muster up enough saliva to talk.

Moments later, they were wailing off down the highway toward the hospital, despite Haley's protestations that she only wanted a ride home.

"We need to get you checked out first," the paramedic explained.

"Can I have some water, please?" she whispered.

"After I check your vitals. We'll get you something to drink just as soon as we can."

Resigned to being forced to jump through the innumerable medical hoops associated with a trip to the hospital, Haley closed her eyes and let the paramedics do their thing.

When they wheeled her through the emergency room doors a short time later, an auburn-haired woman approached her.

"I'm Doctor Nelson," she said flashing a quick smile. "Can you show me where it hurts?"

Haley touched her chest. She was aching all over, but the only real pain was where the airbag had slammed into her.

Doctor Nelson examined her carefully and then listened to her heart with a stethoscope. "Best case scenario, it's only heavy bruising, but I'm going to send you to X-ray as a precaution."

Before Haley had a chance to respond, Jake appeared in the doorway, an anguished expression on his face. "Hales!" He lunged toward her. "Are you all right, sweetheart?"

"I'm fine. My chest hurts from the airbag, that's all."

Jake gently brushed her hair back from her forehead. "What happened?"

Haley sucked on her lip as she rewound the scene in her head. "I was exiting the freeway and the brakes failed. I ended up rear ending the truck in front of me."

A perturbed frown crossed Jake's forehead. "You just had new brake pads put on a month ago."

Haley studied his expression. She could see the doubt creeping over his face. Almost as if he suspected she'd caused the accident, that she'd got distracted, or that lack of sleep had made her reactions slower than usual. She could hardly fault him. She was questioning things herself, sifting through the moments before it had happened in search of answers.

"You can wait here for your wife, if you like," Doctor Nelson said to Jake. "We're taking her to X-ray."

As it turned out, they didn't end up bringing her back to the ER. After reviewing the x-rays, Doctor Nelson determined that she'd fractured a rib. As a precautionary measure, she was being admitted overnight.

"Jake, can you run home and get me some clothes, please?" Haley asked as a hospital attendant wheeled her toward an elevator. "Grab some pajamas, and sweats, and a T-shirt to wear home in the morning. And call Nick for me and let him know I won't be in today." She hesitated and then added, "Be kind to Katniss. She's going to miss me."

Jake kissed her on the forehead. "Don't worry about her, I'll make sure she's well looked after. I need to go in to work for a couple of hours. I'll be back in a little bit to check on you."

After the nursing staff had settled Haley into her room and given her some painkillers, she closed her eyes to rest, but she found herself replaying the accident, yet again, trying to figure out what had happened—if she'd braked in time or reacted too late to the looming truck bed.

A knock on the door roused her from a deep sleep. She glanced up to see a police officer standing in the doorway. Shock detonated through her as she blinked herself awake. How long had she been sleeping? Whatever the nurse had given her had knocked her out cold. She watched warily as the police officer entered the room and pulled up a chair next to her bed. "I'm Detective Tillet," he began. "How are you feeling?"

"Sore. And stupid for rear-ending a truck." Haley pulled a face, trying desperately to ignore her sweating palms—an involuntary physiological reaction that manifested itself any time she crossed paths with a police officer. Every detail of her interview from the day Emma hanged herself came rushing back, every lie she'd told the investigating officers rising up inside her like an accusing finger.

Detective Tillet stretched a sympathetic smile across his face. "I gather from the police report that you applied the brakes repeatedly."

Haley frowned, her pulse throbbing. "Yes, I'm sure I did. I don't understand what happened."

Detective Tillet pulled out a notebook and scribbled

something down. "We had your car towed to a nearby body shop."

Haley groaned. "Not again."

The detective raised an eyebrow. "Another mishap?"

Haley's heart fluttered. She shouldn't have mentioned it. "Well, not exactly. Someone keyed my car a while back. It was no big deal. The passenger door had to be repainted."

To her dismay, Tillet bent over his pad and made a note of it. When he looked up again, his expression was grim. "When was this?"

Haley swatted a hand through the air dismissively. She knew precisely when it had happened—she'd logged the date in her book—but the detective didn't need to know that. "A couple of months ago, probably kids."

"Where did it happen?" Detective Tillet pressed.

Haley shrugged. "To be honest, I'm not sure. I didn't notice it until later in the day. It could have been in the underground parking structure at work, or while I was at the grocery store."

She twiddled her thumbs in front of her. "I hope the damage to my car isn't too bad. I'd prefer not to go through my insurance if at all possible."

Detective Tillet rubbed a finger against his temple pensively. "You'll have to discuss that with the body shop. I'm more concerned about your brakes than the damage to the body of your car."

"I just had new brake pads installed a month ago," Haley said.

Detective Tillet nodded thoughtfully. "Yeah, the technician at the body shop said they looked good. That's not the reason your brakes failed. Turns out there was a small tear in your brake line."

Haley raised her brows. "Oh wow. Maybe I should have a

full service done while my car's in the shop. It's two years old and all I've done so far is change the oil."

"It was a ... precise tear," Detective Tillet continued, scrutinizing her. "The repair technician who spotted it is fairly certain it didn't occur naturally."

Haley's chest heaved up and down, her breathing shallow and sharp. Was she understanding the detective correctly? If it wasn't down to wear and tear, then it wasn't an accident. He was suggesting someone had tampered with her brakes. She curled her toes beneath the sheet, her voice quietening, "That's why you're here, isn't it? You think someone cut my brake line."

"It's a possibility we have to consider, especially in light of the vandalism you mentioned. It was a very small nick, but it appears to have been made by a tool."

Haley dropped her gaze. Her hands shook in her lap as the stark reality of what he was saying hit home. The stalking had suddenly gone way beyond the realm of harassment. Someone had tried to kill her.

"Haley, is there anyone you know who might want to harm you?"

She raised her head and met the detective's perceptive gaze. This wasn't just a sick game, and it wasn't something she could handle on her own anymore. She had no choice but to start at the beginning and tell Detective Tillet everything—everything except her darkest secret.

15

When Haley had finished recounting the harrowing incidents that had occurred over the past six months, Detective Tillet leaned back in his chair and glanced through his notes. "Based on everything you've told me, it sounds like someone has a personal vendetta against you. I'd like to take a look at that logbook you've been keeping for starters. I realize you have your suspicions about who your stalker might be, and we'll certainly make a point of interviewing everyone you identified who had motive and opportunity." He hesitated before adding, "But, I'm going to be blunt about what I need to ask you, so don't jump down my throat. Is there any chance your husband could be behind any of this?"

Haley sighed, letting her shoulders sag. "I really don't think so. I did consider that possibility when things started happening. I mean, he had ample opportunity, and it all began around the time I met him. I even called his work and spoke to the receptionist the day the rotten fruit was delivered to my house. She said he never left the office that afternoon. He was in a quarterly department meeting from lunchtime on." Haley fell silent, wondering if she should mention the fact that her next-door neighbor thought she'd seen a man around Jake's height and weight dropping off the parcel. But Edith was blind as a bat. Haley wasn't about to throw Jake under the bus, not when she already knew for sure he'd been at his office all afternoon.

Detective Tillet gave a sympathetic nod. "That's a start, but it doesn't rule him out entirely. He could have hired someone to deliver the fruit." The detective leaned forward and clasped his hands together in front of him. "I've been doing this a long time, Haley. Unfortunately, in my experience, it often transpires that the spouse is behind this kind of thing. I need you to at least be open to the possibility so you can help us eliminate your husband as a suspect."

"Okay," she said, dubiously. "But I really can't imagine that Jake would do something this heinous. Besides, it's been going on since before we got married. And what would be his motive?"

"Do you have a life insurance policy?"

Haley shrugged. "A small one. A couple of hundred thousand dollars. We both do."

"Has your husband ever been aggressive toward you?"

An image of Jake kicking Katniss flashed to mind. Did he have a hidden cruel streak, or had she simply driven him to the point of frustration by not enforcing the rules they'd agreed upon about keeping Katniss off the couch? Jake had never laid a hand on her, or threatened her in any way, or even yelled at her. On the contrary, he was very even-keeled in his dealings with her, even when she frustrated him—a frustration that was justified of late. "No, he's never been aggressive to me, verbally or physically."

"Good. Are you willing to help us rule him out as a suspect?" Detective Tillet asked.

"I guess." Haley gave a helpless shrug. "What do I need to do?"

"For now, just continue keeping your log and noting down anything odd or suspicious, and your husband's whereabouts each time something happens."

Haley nodded distractedly. "I think you should interview Harold Moore, my next-door neighbor. He had easy access to my car. I leave it parked in my driveway and half the time it's unlocked. He could have gone out in the middle of the night and cut the brake line. And he practically threatened me several weeks ago when I was in his house talking to his sister. She's terrified of him, so that tells you something about what he's capable of."

"We'll send someone around to have a chat with Harold, and the other neighbors in your cul-de-sac. If nothing else, it's possible one of them saw or heard something that could prove helpful." Detective Tillet got to his feet and handed her his card. "Call me if you notice anything suspicious, or if you feel threatened in any way. In the meantime, don't say anything to your husband about the brake line in your car being tampered with. I'll be in touch about taking a look at that logbook you're keeping."

His footsteps faded down the corridor and Haley sank back against her pillows trying to digest the enormity of what he'd told her. Someone wanted her dead. And, whether she liked it or not, the police were involved now. She desperately wanted to talk it over with Jake, but she needed to heed Detective Tillet's warning, at least until he'd eliminated Jake as a suspect. She toyed with the idea of calling her parents, but she couldn't bring herself to alarm them any further than she already had. They might decide to hop on a plane if she told them she was in the hospital.

Reaching out her arm, she managed to hook her fingertips around the strap of her purse lying on the small tray table near the bed. She groaned as she inched it toward her, her chest throbbing with the simple movement. Desperate to talk to someone, she dug out her phone and dialed Natalie's number.

"Hey you," Natalie answered. "I texted you earlier. Where are you?"

"I'm in the hospital," Haley said.

"Are you serious?" Natalie's playful tone switched to one of concern. "What happened?"

"I rear-ended a truck getting off the freeway."

"What? No way! You didn't fall asleep, did you? You've been so tired lately."

"No, nothing like that. My brakes failed." Haley paused mid-thought and chewed on her lip, debating whether or not to tell Natalie the truth. Detective Tillet had only warned her not to mention it to Jake. And she badly wanted to get Natalie's take on things. It couldn't do any harm. "The thing is, Nats, a detective stopped by here a few minutes ago. He told me the body shop discovered a suspicious tear in the brake line."

Natalie let out a gasp. "You mean … are you saying someone deliberately tampered with your brakes?"

"That's what this Detective Tillet thinks. I filled him in on everything else that's been happening too. He's going to send someone around to talk to my neighbor, Harold Moore—the scary hoarder."

"Good! It's about time someone put an end to this. It's gone on long enough."

Haley said nothing for a moment. Natalie was right. If someone didn't put an end to it soon, it might end with her demise. It was a sobering thought.

"You still there, Hales?"

"Yeah."

"What's wrong?" Natalie pressed. "There's something else

you're not telling me, isn't there? You should know by now you can't hide anything from me."

Haley furrowed her brow. "I hate even bringing this up, but I think the detective suspects Jake. He kept going on about how it's usually the spouse who's behind things like this. He even asked about our life insurance policies."

Natalie let out a snort. "He doesn't know Jake. It's his job to consider everyone in your immediate circle a suspect. It's protocol. Process of elimination. Don't worry about it. He'll probably question me too."

"He wants me to keep documenting everything and confirm Jake's whereabouts each time something happens. I told him Jake was at his office when the rotten fruit was delivered, but he said Jake could have hired someone to drop it off for him."

"That's ridiculous," Natalie protested. "Why would Jake do that? Unless you have some kind of multimillion-dollar insurance policy or some—" She caught herself mid-sentence and then continued, "*Do* you?"

"No, of course not. We each have a two-hundred-thousand-dollar policy, that's it. Barely enough to pay off the house."

"Hardly enough to kill for," Natalie mused. "Unless Jake has debts you don't know about."

"No, we have joint accounts. He doesn't hide anything from me."

"Well then, there's your answer. I'm sure the cops just need to rule him out. As soon as they've done that, they'll get busy finding the jerk who's doing this to you."

"I hope so," Haley said. "I'm not sure how much more of this I can take." She glanced up at the sound of footsteps to see Jake entering her room with a duffel bag in hand. Her grip on the phone tightened involuntarily. "I gotta go, Nats.

Jake just arrived. Thanks for chatting." She ended the call and slipped her phone back inside her purse.

Jake set down the duffle bag and smiled. "How are you feeling?"

"It hurts to breathe hard. Other than that, I'm okay."

Jake slid into the chair Detective Tillet had vacated moments earlier and reached for Haley's hand. He interlaced his fingers with hers in the familiar comforting way he had done from the very beginning of their relationship. "I'm so sorry, Hales. I haven't been supporting you like you deserve. I should have believed you from the outset."

She squeezed his hands lightly, wondering as she did if these were the hands that had cut her brake line. A tiny shiver crossed her shoulders. "I haven't been the woman you married lately either. I've been falling apart at the seams. I can understand your frustration with me."

Jake raised her fingers to his lips and kissed them gently. "I want that woman back, and I'll do anything to make it happen."

"I know," she said softly. "Your efforts haven't gone unnoticed. After all, you caved in and let me get Katniss and a cutting-edge security system."

Jake chuckled. "Speaking of Katniss, she whined like a baby when I packed your clothes. I swear she knew you weren't coming home tonight." He reached into his pocket and fished out his phone. "Here, I took a picture of her so you can see how miserable she is without you."

Haley studied the shot of Katniss with her head resting on her paws, staring morosely at the camera. "Poor baby. I feel so bad for her." She handed the phone back to Jake. "I'll make it up to her when I get home tomorrow."

"You'll have to be careful with your broken rib," Jake warned her. "She's going to be especially rambunctious when she sees you again."

"I know." Haley let out a weary sigh. "She won't understand why I can't play with her."

"I'll volunteer to be your temporary stand-in," Jake offered. "She doesn't like me half as much, but at least I can throw the ball to her in the backyard."

"Thank you, babe. That's sweet of you," Haley answered, touched by the gesture, knowing how little affection Jake had for dog hair and slobber.

He rubbed a hand across his jaw. "Do you want me to call the body shop and get an estimate on your car?"

"No!" Haley said, a little too abruptly. "I mean, I'll sort it out with the insurance company. They're going to need my authorization anyway."

Jake shrugged. "Whatever. Just trying take some of the load off you."

Haley leaned forward and kissed him on the lips. "I know. And I appreciate it. You're the best."

"I should get going and let you rest," Jake said. "I brought a stack of work home I need to tackle."

"Don't forget you promised to play with Katniss. I'm going to ask her if you followed through."

"I'm on it," he said, winking at her.

Haley yawned. "I slept hard after I got to my room, but I'm still wiped out. I feel like a dishrag after this whole ordeal."

Jake wrinkled his brow. "Do you think you got distracted or something?"

"I guess so," Haley replied offhandedly. "I was mulling over all the work stacked up on my desk. I must have spaced out and not noticed the truck in front of me braking."

Jake's expression relaxed. "Don't stress out about it anymore. I know you haven't been sleeping well lately. I'm just glad the accident wasn't serious and that you're okay."

"Thanks." Haley forced herself to smile as he blew her a kiss before exiting the room.

She closed her eyes and let out a relieved breath at his departure, leaving her alone with her conflicted thoughts. *Was* he glad she was okay? If he wasn't, he was an impressive actor. But she was a good actress too—she'd had plenty of practice over the years. She'd done as Detective Tillet requested and kept Jake in the dark about the damaged brake line. If she was in any danger from her husband, she didn't want him to know she was watching him now too.

16

A few weeks after her accident, Haley was fast asleep in bed in the middle of the night when she woke with a start. She blinked, listening for the sound that had startled her. *Footsteps.* Was that what she'd heard? Or was she dreaming?

She reached out a hand and felt Jake's warm, motionless body next to her. She listened to his even breathing for several minutes as she lay beneath the duvet, silent and frozen still, alert to any movement. It couldn't be Katniss she'd heard moving around. Haley had dropped her off that morning to get spayed and the vet had kept her overnight after she'd reacted badly to the anesthesia. Just when she was about to turn over and go back to sleep, a floorboard creaked. Her body tensed, her blood oddly cold in her veins. A strange prickling sensation came over her. What if her stalker was in the house? Gripped with fear, she jabbed Jake in the back. "Jake!" she hissed. "Wake up!"

He groaned and shifted in the bed, then rubbed his eyes and peered over at her. "What? What's going on?" His voice was lethargic, heavy with sleep.

"Someone's in the house," Haley whispered urgently. "I heard them walking around."

"Come on, Hales. It's two o'clock in the morning. Go back to sleep."

"I'm serious, Jake. Someone is moving around out there—they stepped on that loose board outside the guest bedroom."

He yawned loudly and rolled over. "Katniss would have barked if someone was in the house."

"She's not here. She's still at the vet's, remember?"

Jake groaned again, tossed aside the duvet and tumbled out of bed. "All right, I'll check it out, but I'm telling you there's no one in the house."

"Please be careful, Jake!" Haley sat up in bed and pulled the duvet up to her neck. She hadn't imagined it. She'd heard a floorboard creak. There was one spot in particular on their landing near the guest bedroom that always made a squeaking sound when anyone walked on it. Agonizing minutes ticked by before Jake returned. He threw himself back down on the bed and curled up beneath the duvet with a shiver. "You're mistaken. There's no one there, no ghosts or zombies wandering around in the house. You must have been dreaming."

Haley pressed her knuckles to her forehead. *Could* she have imagined it? Maybe it wasn't the floorboard—just the house settling or something. Despite the sleeping pill she'd taken, she'd slept fitfully, but the creak that had wakened her was an all-too-familiar sound. "I'm sure I wasn't dreaming, Jake. It sounded like someone was walking around out there. What about the cameras? Did you check them?"

"They need to be reset," he mumbled. "The power went out when I was watching TV."

"Are you kidding me?" Haley exclaimed. "Why didn't you do it before you came to bed? You know how important that is."

She waited for him to respond but he was already snoring.

She didn't sleep a wink for the rest of the night, convinced someone had been in their house. One of the neighbors, perhaps? The same neighbor who'd thrown out her wok. She tossed and turned, speculating if it might have been Harold. But how had he got inside? Her thoughts turned to Stan. She'd always wondered at the back of her mind if he'd kept a key to their house after showing it. It wouldn't be ethical, but unethical people didn't do things by the book. And then there was Jim—as a handyman, it wouldn't be hard for him to find a way into their house. She didn't know too much about Anthony, but Jake had mentioned that he was obsessed with online gaming—up at all hours of the night—which was enough to make him a suspect as far as she was concerned.

Shortly before dawn, Haley slipped out of bed and wandered down to the kitchen. She made herself a strong pot of coffee and sat down at the table, sliding her fingers around her mug to warm them. She might as well go into the office early and start on the stack of work piled up on her desk. Only yesterday, Nick had expressed concern about her growing backlog. It was the first time she'd come dangerously close to letting him down on a case deadline. She needed to make things right before he lost faith in her.

With a heavy sigh she picked up her mug to take a sip of coffee—and froze.

A face in a black ski mask was pressed up against the kitchen window. The mug slipped from her fingers, smashing on the tile below, coffee splattering in every direction. She shoved her chair back, yelping as the hot liquid splashed her ankles. She stared down at the mess in disbelief before glancing back up at the kitchen window. The face was gone! A cold sweat spread over her shoulders. Was it her stalker? What if he tried to get inside the house? She kept her eyes trained on the window and rubbed her temples trying to collect her thoughts. Had she actually seen a face or had she imagined it? After all, she'd barely slept. Her eyes were burning, and her brain was a complete fog. She briefly considered waking Jake, but he already thought she'd been dreaming when she heard the footsteps last night. He'd think she'd lost it entirely if she told him she'd seen a face at the window and it turned out there was no one prowling around outside.

She reached for her purse on the counter and rummaged through it for Detective Tillet's card, staring at the number for a moment. He'd urged her to call if anything else happened. He suspected her husband was behind the harassment, but this proved otherwise. Jake was fast asleep in bed last night when she'd heard the footsteps. It seemed ludicrous to think he would hire someone to walk around inside their house or peer in the window just to scare her. Still, whoever the intruder was, he knew Katniss wouldn't be here. It couldn't be merely a coincidence. Her intruder knew her schedule. Before she could talk herself out of it, she pulled out her phone and punched in Detective Tillet's number. Maybe he could send a cop over to take a quick look and check for footprints at least—any evidence at all to prove she wasn't going mad.

"Detective Tillet speaking."

"Hi, it's Haley Wilder."

"Is everything okay?"

"No, not really. That's why I'm calling. I heard someone walking around in my house last night. Jake thinks I'm losing it, but I didn't imagine it. I heard the floorboard outside the guest bedroom creak."

There was a slight pause before Detective Tillet asked, "Did you see anyone?"

"No," she admitted. "But, I spotted someone outside the house. I got up early to make a pot of coffee and when I sat down at the table, there was a face in a ski mask pressed up against the kitchen window. I think it was a man, but I'm not sure."

"What time was that at?"

"Just a few minutes ago. He scared me half to death. I spilled my coffee everywhere."

"Did you check to make sure your doors are locked?"

Haley bit her lip. "No, I … assumed they were. We always lock them before we go to bed."

"Stay on the line with me while you check," Detective Tillet said, an edge of heightened concern in his voice.

Haley got to her feet and checked the door off the kitchen first. "The back door's locked," she confirmed.

"Okay, now try the front one."

She swallowed hard as she made her way down the hall toward the front door, half-expecting a man in a ski mask to burst through at any second. "It's locked," she said in a relieved whisper.

"Good," Detective Tillet responded. "I've dispatched a patrol car to your house. I'll have my officer check the perimeter to make sure no one's loitering outside. I'll stay on the phone with you until the patrol car gets there so I can confirm the officer's identity. You'll need to give him a statement."

"All right." Haley gave a resigned sigh. "But please ask him not to ring the doorbell. Jake's still asleep." With a bit of luck, he'd stay asleep and he wouldn't find out that she'd called Detective Tillet. He'd be annoyed with her for making a fuss, but just because he hadn't seen anyone didn't mean there hadn't been an intruder in their house last night—or loitering around outside this morning.

"I need to set down the phone for a minute while I clean up the mess I made," Haley said. "I'll put you on speaker."

"Go right ahead," Detective Tillet replied. "I'm here if you need me."

Haley fetched a dustpan and broom and began sweeping up the broken pieces of the mug, and then got a rag and mopped up the coffee as best she could. She needed to get rid of the evidence of her hysteria before Jake came downstairs and freaked out about the mess all over the tile floor.

A short time later, she heard a car pull up outside the house. "The police officer's here," she said to Detective Tillet. She peered through the family room curtain at the squad car, wondering if Edith, or Harold, was doing the same thing next door. More drama for them to gossip about. A young police officer exited the car, walked around the side of the house and then reappeared a few minutes later at the front door. He knocked gently, and held up his ID. "His name's Wheatley," Haley said into the phone.

"That's him. You can let him in," Detective Tillett responded. "I'm going to hang up now."

Haley set down her phone and opened the door.

"I'm Officer Wheatley," the man said, inclining his head. "Detective Tillet sent me to do a welfare check. He briefed me on what's been going on. I understand you heard an intruder and saw someone outside your window."

"Yes, come on in." Haley led him through to the kitchen and indicated for him to take a seat.

"I see you have a security system. Have you checked your camera footage yet?" Officer Wheatley asked.

Haley grimaced. "The power went out earlier this evening. The cameras need to be reset."

Officer Wheatley pressed his lips into a disapproving line as he fished out a notebook from his pocket. "Can you tell me what time you heard the intruder walking around inside your house?"

Before Haley had a chance to answer, Jake appeared in the doorway, still in his pajamas, a look of utter confusion on his face. "What's going on?"

"I saw someone outside our house," Haley explained hastily. "He had his face pressed up against the kitchen window and he was staring in at me. It could have been the intruder. I knew I wasn't dreaming when I heard footsteps inside the house last night."

Jake scratched his head and wordlessly joined them at the table. He folded his arms over his chest and waited for Haley to continue.

She turned her attention back to Officer Wheatley. "It was a little after three this morning when I heard someone prowling around outside our room. My husband got up to take a look, but he didn't see anyone."

Officer Wheatley turned to Jake. "No sign of forced entry?"

Jake shook his head. "None, I couldn't find any evidence that anyone had been in the house. Nothing was disturbed."

Officer Wheatley jotted down a few notes and then turned his attention back to Haley. "What time did you see the face pressed up against the kitchen window?"

"Around five-fifteen. I made some coffee and sat down at the kitchen table with it. When I looked up, someone was leaning against the glass staring right at me."

"Can you give me a description?"

"Not really, I think it was a man. He was wearing a ski mask so I couldn't see his face. But I'd say he was at least five-ten." She hesitated. "Did you find any footprints out there?"

"Nothing," Officer Wheatley said. "But that doesn't mean to say there wasn't anyone out there. It hasn't rained in a couple of weeks, so the ground isn't damp, and there's a concrete pathway right outside your kitchen window."

Jake turned to Haley. "Don't you think it's possible you might have imagined it, sweetheart? You hardly slept all night. Your mind could have been playing tricks on you."

Haley frowned and dropped her gaze. Loathe as she was to admit it, she was beginning to ask herself the same question now that the sun was up. Could she have imagined it in her sleep-deprived state?

Officer Wheatley cleared his throat. "I'll write up this report and pass it along to Detective Tillet. I understand this is part of an ongoing investigation."

Jake frowned and pinned a questioning gaze on Haley. "What's he talking about?"

Her cheeks heated as she wrestled with how much to tell him, Detective Tillet's warning still rang in her ears. "I decided to file a police report on the vandalism to my car. Probably not a big deal, but I thought it wouldn't do any harm to have it on record—that and the other stuff that's been happening."

The expression on Jake's face hardened. "And you didn't think it was worthwhile telling me? Or were you trying to keep it from me?"

Officer Wheatley scratched the back of his neck and stood, looking decidedly uncomfortable. "I'll see myself out."

"Thanks for coming by," Haley said. "I really appreciate it." She got to her feet and accompanied him to the front door, casting a quick glance over her shoulder to make sure Jake couldn't overhear her. "My husband thinks I'm imagining things, but someone was in our house last night, I'm sure of it."

Officer Wheatley gave a respectful nod. "You might want to think about staying with a friend for a couple of nights. If the intruder returns, you may not be so lucky next time."

17

*H*aley remained subdued at work that day. She put on a good show of being absorbed in the assignments Nick had told her to prioritize, but in reality her mind kept backtracking through the events of the previous night. The thud of the intruder's footsteps replayed on a continual loop in her head. On several occasions during the course of the morning, she found herself retreating to the bathroom on the verge of a full-blown panic attack. Her chest hurt and her palms were sweaty, but most disconcerting of all was that she was having a hard time getting her breathing under control. Each time, she splashed cold water on her face and sank down with her back against the bathroom wall, praying no one would walk in on her until she felt sufficiently composed to return to her desk. Truth be told, it felt like she was dying. It was bad enough to know that someone was stalking her, but the thought that they'd been inside her house was more than she could handle.

Somehow, she struggled through until lunchtime. Natalie took one look at her and grimaced. "Lunch is on me. I know you've got something preying on your mind."

"I've got too much to do," Haley protested, throwing a quick look Nick's way as he exited his office with a new client in tow. "I need to work through lunch today. I can't risk slipping behind again."

"You're not going to accomplish anything unless you get whatever's bothering you off your chest," Natalie replied. "I'm not taking no for an answer. We won't be gone long."

Reluctantly, Haley closed up the binder on her desk, picked up her purse, and followed Natalie into the elevator. If nothing else, she could use some fresh air to clear her head.

Natalie pressed the button for the lower level. "What are you in the mood for?"

Haley shrugged. "Anything. I'm not even hungry."

Natalie shook her head in disbelief. "First you can't sleep, now you can't eat. What's going on with you?"

Before Haley could respond, the elevator dinged, and the doors opened in the underground parking structure.

"Hold that thought," Natalie said briskly. "You can tell me everything over lunch."

Ten minutes later, they slipped into a high-backed leather booth at Al Forno, a local Italian restaurant that offered a quiet, intimate atmosphere and served excellent pizza.

"You have to eat something," Natalie insisted, eying the menu as the tantalizing smell of a rich seafood pasta dish wafted their way from the next booth.

Haley placed her elbows on the table and rested her head in her hands. "Just order a pizza. Any vegetarian one. I'll split it with you."

When the waiter came by, Natalie selected a smoked eggplant and basil pizza and ordered an iced tea for herself.

"Diet Coke for me," Haley said. "I need the caffeine."

Moments later, one of the wait staff appeared with a platter of homemade bread and dipping oil and placed it on the table.

"So," Natalie said, tearing off a hunk of bread and arching a brow at Haley. "What's going on? Did something else happen?"

Haley shivered, the sound of a creaking floor board echoing in her aching head.

Natalie appraised her with concern. "Are you cold? Or are you coming down with something?"

"Someone was in my house last night," Haley blurted out.

Natalie's eyes narrowed. "What do you mean?"

"An intruder—walking around upstairs."

"What?" Natalie threw a quick glance around the restaurant and then leaned in closer. "Did you catch him?"

"No. I heard the floor board creaking outside the guest bedroom. By the time I woke Jake up and sent him out to take a look, the intruder had gone."

Natalie blinked and sat back in her chair digesting the news. "How do you know for sure there was someone in your house? I mean, I'm not doubting that you heard the floor board creaking, but sometimes houses make weird noises."

Haley shook her head. "Somebody definitely walked across that floor board, it makes a very distinctive sound. And that's not all. I couldn't get back to sleep so I went down to the kitchen around five or so to make coffee. When I sat down at the table, I saw a face pressed up against the window staring in at me."

Natalie clapped a hand to her mouth, her eyes widening in alarm. "Did you recognize him?"

"No, he was wearing a ski mask. I assume it was a man— he was fairly tall."

"Did you set Katniss on him?"

"She wasn't there," Haley explained. "I had her spayed yesterday and she had a bad reaction to the anesthesia, so the vet kept her overnight. It can't be a coincidence.

Someone knew our movements and struck while the dog was gone."

"Did Jake see the face at the window?"

"No, he was asleep. I called Detective Tillet, and he sent an officer over. He searched around the perimeter of the house but he didn't see any sign of anyone. He took my statement though." Haley's voice trailed off as the waiter approached with their order.

He set down their pizza with a flourish. "Anything else I can get you ladies?"

"No, thank you," Haley said, squeezing her lips into a smile. "This looks great."

Natalie reached for a slice of pizza and took a large bite. "Yum, this place makes the best thin crust ever."

Haley stared at the sizzling pizza, her stomach recoiling at the thought of food.

Natalie lifted a piece and slapped it down on Haley's plate. "Eat!" she commanded her. "You're going to waste away. I'm not having it."

Haley lifted the pizza to her lips and took a tentative bite, hoping she could keep it down.

For the next few minutes, they focused on their food, the silence interspersed with Natalie's appreciative moans. She let out a satisfied sigh and wiped her lips with her napkin. "So, are the police going to follow up on the intruder? Interview your neighbors again?"

"I'm not sure," Haley responded. "Detective Tillet already paid Harold a visit last week. He claims he only left the house a handful of times in the past year. I don't think Detective Tillet really believes he's the stalker. And I tend to agree. Harold's mean-spirited enough to carry out some of the things that have happened, but he's overweight and unfit. It would be hard for him to move around undetected."

"So who do you think is behind it?" Natalie asked.

Haley pondered the question for a minute. "I haven't ruled out everyone in my cul-de-sac yet. Like I told you before, there's a possibility Stan might still have a key to our house. That makes me uncomfortable."

Natalie wrinkled her brow. "But what motive would he have to stalk you?"

"I don't know." Haley threw up her hands despairingly. "I don't understand how stalkers think. Maybe they just get a kick out of tormenting people." The words hung in the air, the irony not lost on her. She'd been that person once, getting a kick out of making life miserable for others. Except deep down she hadn't enjoyed it, she just hadn't had the backbone to stand up to Lachlan.

"Does Detective Tillet still think Jake might be behind it?" Natalie asked.

"He hasn't ruled him out yet," Haley said. "But Jake was asleep in the bed next to me when I heard the prowler."

"So, what are you going to do?"

"Call a locksmith and have the locks changed, for starters. I meant to do it this morning, but I got snowed under with work." Haley sighed. "The officer who came by suggested that we stay with friends for a couple of nights in case the stalker comes back."

"You're welcome to bunk with me if you want," Natalie offered, taking a sip of her iced tea.

"Thanks, but Jake would never agree to it. Besides, Katniss will be home tonight. I'm picking her up after work." Haley poked at a piece of eggplant on her plate. "Actually, I've been thinking about signing up for a self-defense class. At the end of the day, I can't count on Jake or Katniss to protect me. It's not like someone can be with me twenty-four-seven."

"That's a good idea," Natalie said. "Want me to go with you?"

Haley tweaked a smile. "Would you?"

"Sure, why not? Maybe the instructor will be hot."

They dissolved into laughter and Haley reached for another slice of pizza. "My appetite's returning. No sense in letting this go to waste."

Feeling heartened by Natalie's offer to accompany her to self-defense classes, Haley was finally able to concentrate on her work after lunch and take care of the most critical matters Nick needed on his desk by day's end. In between, she found the time to make a quick call to a locksmith who agreed to come out first thing in the morning. When the office closed for the day, Haley packed up her things and walked over to Natalie's desk. "There's a martial arts studio just down the street that offers self-defense classes. Do you want to swing by and check it out?"

Natalie shrugged. "Why not? Now's as good a time as ever."

Haley texted Jake to let him know she'd arranged for a locksmith to come in the morning, and to remind him that she was going to pick up Katniss after work and would be home late. She didn't mention the fact that she was going to sign up for a self defense class. Jake would think she was overreacting and try to talk her out of it.

She plugged the studio address into her GPS and exited the parking lot with Natalie following behind. They pulled up outside Eagle Martial Arts a short time later and headed into the building. To Haley's surprise, the studio took up the entire first floor. They approached the front desk, a simple, but sleek, black counter with a solitary monitor. Behind it, a short, stocky, dark-haired man dressed in a white martial arts jacket and pants was typing on a keyboard. He got to his feet when he saw them and bowed in greeting.

"Welcome, my name is Koki. I'm one of the instructors here. Can I answer any questions for you?"

Haley threw Natalie a discreet glance, trying not to laugh.

He wasn't exactly hot, but, if nothing else, he was polite and cordial.

"We'd like some information about your self-defense classes for women," Haley said.

"We currently have openings on Tuesdays and Thursdays from seven until eight-thirty in the evening. The instructor's name is Haruki. I can introduce you if you like. He's in the office out back taking care of some paperwork."

"What's the cost per class?" Haley inquired.

"Ninety dollars for a semi-private, so forty-five each," Koki answered. "Would you like a quick tour of the studio?"

"Sure," Natalie said, looking at Haley who nodded in confirmation.

"I just need to leave in time to pick up Katniss before the vet closes at seven."

Koki trotted out from behind the desk and indicated for them to follow him as he made his way toward the mats in the middle of the high-ceilinged space where a group of students were going through their paces.

"They're warming up with alternating ankle flexes," Koki explained. "And that's a stride punch the instructor is demonstrating."

After watching for a few minutes, Koki led them away from the mats. "On the back wall here, we have our safety equipment—full-size kick shields and hand-held pads."

Haley eyed them warily. "Will we be needing those?"

"More than likely." Koki beamed at her. "We don't want to incapacitate you during training, kind of defeats the purpose of what we're doing here. Let's continue back this way. Restrooms are on the left, also cubbies and lockers to stash shoes and valuables." He led them down a short corridor. "And here's our office. Haruki can register you if you're ready to sign up."

He gestured for them to go ahead of him.

Natalie and Haley stepped into the cramped but neat office space. The man behind the desk got to his feet and bowed. "My name is Haruki. I'm very pleased to meet you."

They introduced themselves and sat down while Koki bowed and excused himself.

"Which class are you interested in?" Haruki asked.

"A semi-private self-defense class," Haley responded.

"Excellent." Haruki reached for some forms and passed one each to Natalie and Haley, along with a couple of pens. "Go ahead and fill out all the information and make a note of any medical conditions. I'm sure Koki mentioned already that we have openings on Tuesdays and Thursdays. Is there a particular day that works better for you?"

"We'd like to get started right away," Haley said. "Next Tuesday would be great."

Haruki nodded. "I typically recommend at least four sessions to get a good grasp of the techniques."

"That sounds great," Natalie said, glancing up from her paperwork.

Haley filled out her details and listed Jake as her emergency contact, hoping he wouldn't need to be called for any reason. When she got to the last question at the bottom of the form, she hesitated.

What prompted you to sign up for self-defense classes today?

She debated writing something innocuous. Did she really want to divulge why she was here? Would Haruki even believe her?

Natalie set down her pen with a flourish and handed over her paperwork.

Haley hurriedly set about answering the final question before passing her form to Haruki.

He glanced over it and then stared keenly at Haley. "You have a stalker?"

Haley gave a grim nod. "Yes."

Haruki scrutinized her for a moment, as if deliberating over something. He set down the forms and blinked solemnly. "You need to understand that my class is no substitute for a weapon. If you are in imminent danger, I strongly recommend more drastic measures to protect yourself. This isn't the first time I've encountered a situation like this, and unfortunately it didn't end well."

18

*N*atalie and Haley exited the martial arts studio, somewhat shaken by Haruki's warning.

"He's right, you know," Natalie said. "This isn't going to stop your stalker."

"Maybe not, but it can't do any harm to learn a few techniques to defend myself. Every woman should take a class like this."

"I hope I don't make a total fool of myself," Natalie confided.

"You'll do fine. Knowing me, I'll be the dork," Haley reassured her.

"What will Jake think?"

"I'm not going to tell him. Not yet at least. He already thinks I'm paranoid and taking all this too far." Haley gave a rueful shrug. "I'll say I'm taking a fitness class with you. It's close enough to the truth."

Natalie nodded thoughtfully. "That might be for the best. I hate to even go there, but if Detective Tillet's right and it turns out Jake is behind what's been happening to you, then he has no business knowing that you've been learning how to defend yourself."

"I'm not taking self-defense classes to protect myself from my husband," Haley retorted. "He wasn't the one prowling around in our house the other night." She twisted her lips. "Besides, if he ever laid a hand on me, Katniss would take him down in a heartbeat." She glanced at her phone to check the time. "Speaking of which, I need to pick her up. I'll catch you tomorrow."

When Haley pulled up at the vet's office a few minutes later, Katniss was overjoyed to see her, and she had a hard time discouraging her from jumping up and bursting her stitches.

"She needs to lay low for a week or two," the veterinarian assistant explained. "No chasing madly after balls around the garden or anything of that nature."

"What about food?" Haley asked. "Can she eat normally?"

"Yes, she's doing much better today. She's been eating well so no restrictions on that front."

After settling the bill, Haley helped Katniss into the back seat of her 4Runner and chatted to her on the way home. Katniss pricked up her ears every so often when they passed a truck, but for the most part, she was content to lay her head on her paws and listen to Haley ramble.

At seven forty-five, she pulled into the driveway and parked behind Jake's car. She helped Katniss out, and then walked her around to the backyard to let her sniff about and take care of business, before unlocking the back door and stepping into the kitchen. The house was bathed in darkness. She set down her purse and frowned. Maybe Jake had gone out for a drink with a friend. After all, she'd told him she was would be home late. "Jake! Are you here, babe?"

At her side, Katniss emitted a low growl at the back of her throat. Haley threw her an alarmed look. Her heart began to pound with fear. Was there someone in the house again? "What is it, Katniss?" she whispered. She glanced across at the door leading out of the kitchen into the shadowy hallway. Where was Jake?

Suddenly, all her doubts about him came rushing back. Detective Tillet's warning echoed in her ears. Was her husband waiting to ambush her in the dark? It was a ridiculous idea, but she couldn't shake her misgivings as she listened in the darkness for the sound of someone moving around. Why wasn't he answering her?

She glanced around looking for something she could use as a weapon. Eyes alighting on the knife block on the counter, she quietly slid out the largest blade. Too bad she hadn't taken a couple of self-defense classes already. She couldn't count on Katniss in her weakened condition to be of any help. Gingerly, she crept over to the door and peered around it into the darkened hallway. Closing the kitchen door behind her to make sure Katniss didn't follow her, she padded softly over to the family room and peeked inside. The shadowy space was deserted, and nothing appeared to be disturbed.

Silently, she crept toward the stairs. Quaking with fear, she began to climb to the second floor. Avoiding the creaky floor board outside the guest bedroom, she tiptoed toward the master bedroom. The door was ajar, but the room was cloaked in darkness, just like the rest of the house. Cautiously, she stuck her head inside, poised and ready to strike at any intruder. Her eyes widened, blood draining from her head at the shocking sight.

Her husband lay motionless on the floor at the foot of their bed.

"Jake!" she shrieked. Tossing the knife aside, she shoved the bedroom door wide open and dropped to her knees at his side. "Jake! Jake, can you hear me?" She shook him gently, then frantically felt for a pulse. Relief flooded through her. He was breathing. Her fingers scrabbled for her phone.

"911, what is your emergency?"

"My ... my husband," she blubbered. "He's ... I just got home. He's lying on the floor in our bedroom. He's unconscious."

"Is he breathing?"

"Yes, but he's not saying anything. It's bad. Can you send an ambulance? Please, hurry!"

"The ambulance is on its way, ma'am. Can you confirm your address for me?"

"42 Springfield Place."

"And what's your husband's name?"

"Jake, Jake Wilder. I'm his wife, Haley. Please, hurry!"

"Haley, does your husband have any visible injuries?"

"I ... I don't know. There's no blood. I'm not sure."

"How old is your husband?"

"He's thirty-four."

"Okay, Haley. The ambulance will be pulling onto your street in a couple of minutes. Can you open up the front door for the paramedics, please?"

"Yes." She tore her eyes away from Jake's unmoving body, scrambled to her feet and hurried down the stairs. Flashing blue lights assailed her as she flung open the door. "The ambulance is here," she croaked into the phone.

"I'm going to hang up now, Haley," the dispatcher said. "The emergency responders will take it from here."

Haley led the two paramedics upstairs and watched through a haze of turmoil as they did a preliminary examination to determine the extent of Jake's injuries. "Contusion to the back of the head," one of them said, placing an oxygen mask over his face. "Let's get him out of here."

"Can I ride in the ambulance with him?" Haley asked,

clutching the stair rail for support as she followed the paramedics.

"Yes, ma'am, you can sit up front in the passenger seat."

Haley struggled to put the pieces together as the ambulance raced toward the hospital. Someone had struck Jake on the back of the head. The intruder must have come back—looking for her. Jake wasn't the intended victim, he'd simply been in the wrong place at the wrong time. Her heart ached for him. He'd borne the brunt of a vicious attack designed for her. At least now he wouldn't be able to discount what was happening anymore. Her stalker had tried to kill her, *twice*—and he'd almost killed her husband in the process. She buried her face in her hands, overcome with emotion, trying not to lose it entirely.

At the hospital, the trauma team kicked into gear, buzzing around Jake and barking out orders.

"Your husband has suffered blunt force trauma to the back of the head," the ER doctor explained to Haley. "Our first priority is to make sure there's no swelling to the brain."

Despite her best intentions, tears began to stream down her face as it hit home how close she'd come to losing Jake. "We had an intruder in the house the other night," she said. "He must have come back."

The doctor frowned. "Have you notified the police?"

"Yes, I made a report at the time. They've opened an investigation."

"I'd like you to call the detective in charge right away," the doctor replied. "We're obligated to report this kind of injury as suspicious. But if you already have someone working on the case, it would be helpful to bring him up to speed."

Haley nodded glumly. She watched as an orderly wheeled Jake away for an x-ray and MRI, and then pulled out her phone and dialed.

"Detective Tillet speaking."

"It's Haley Wilder," she said, her voice cracking. "I'm at the hospital."

"Are you all right?" he asked in a grim tone.

"I'm fine. It's my husband, Jake. Someone hit him on the back of the head and knocked him out. I found him lying on our bedroom floor when I got home this evening."

"I'm on my way. I'll send a team to your house and have it processed as a crime scene."

"Thank you," Haley said, sinking into a chair, energy seeping from her bones as the magnitude of what had happened hit her.

Twenty minutes later, Detective Tillet strode into the ER, accompanied by a female police officer. He pulled his brows together in concern when he spotted Haley. "Any word on your husband?"

"He's not back from the MRI yet." She rubbed her arms nervously. "I guess this rules him out as a suspect. I can't imagine he was able to whack himself on the back of the head and hide the weapon before he passed out."

Detective Tillet grimaced. "I admit that would be hard to accomplish. Do you have a key to your house that I can give my officer?"

"Sure," Haley said, rummaging around in her purse. "Oddly enough, I just set up an appointment to have the locks changed tomorrow morning. It's as if the stalker knows my every move." She retrieved her key and passed it to the officer. "By the way, my German shepherd's in the kitchen. She was spayed yesterday so she's not supposed to get excited or jump around or anything."

The woman gave a nod of acknowledgement. "We'll bear that in mind, ma'am."

Detective Tillet issued a few more instructions to the police officer before she took off, and then turned to Haley. "Do you know what time Jake got home from work today?"

"No, I went to run a couple of errands after work, so I was late getting back. It was almost eight o'clock." She swallowed a small sob. "He could have been lying on the floor for hours for all I know."

"Mrs. Wilder?"

Haley glanced up to see the ER doctor striding back into the room, his expression unreadable. She half rose out of her chair, terrified of the news he was about to deliver.

"Your husband has regained consciousness. He's asking for you. I'm happy to report that the MRI shows no bleeding on the brain and no skull fracture. He'll likely have a decent-sized knot on his head for a week or so, and a concussion. He has no recollection of what happened, but apart from that he's going to be just fine."

Haley let out a shuddering sigh of relief. "Thank you so much. Can I see him now?"

"Of course." The doctor flashed her a cursory smile. "I'll have an orderly escort you to his room. We're admitting him overnight as a precaution."

Haley turned to Detective Tillet. "Do you want to speak to him?"

He gave a curt nod. "I'll need to take his statement, even if he can't remember much. Rest assured, I'll be bumping up the priority on your case after tonight."

He accompanied her and the orderly into the elevator and up to the third floor where Jake had been admitted into a semi-private room.

Haley ran to her husband's bedside and threw her arms around him, sobbing against his chest. Remorse that she'd ever suspected him of trying to hurt her overwhelmed her. "Oh Jake, I'm so glad you're all right."

"I'm sorry I ever doubted you," he replied weakly.

Detective Tillet waited at a respectful distance until Haley had disentangled herself. He shook Jake's hand and introduced himself, and then sat down in a chair next to the bed. "I'm Detective Tillet. We haven't met yet, but I've been working on your wife's case."

"Thank you," Jake croaked. He winced as he adjusted his position on the pillow. "I have to admit I've been skeptical about the whole stalker thing at times. I was flat wrong."

Detective Tillet pulled out his notebook. "Did you manage to get a look at your assailant?"

Jake drew his brows together in concentration. "No, he struck me from behind."

"He?" Detective Tillet echoed.

"Well, I assume it was a man—Haley thought it was a man's face at the kitchen window the other morning."

"And you didn't hear him approaching?" Detective Tillet pressed.

"No, he was hiding behind the bedroom door."

"Any sign of forced entry when you arrived home?"

"Not that I noticed." Jake furrowed his brow. "I came in the front door. It was locked."

"The back door was locked too," Haley interjected. "I went in that way."

Detective Tillet grimaced. "I think it's safe to assume the intruder has a key to your house. You need to call an emergency locksmith and get those locks changed tonight—it can't wait until morning." He tapped his pen on his notebook. "Are your cameras working properly now?"

"As far as I know," Haley replied. "Unless the intruder deactivated them."

Detective Tillet pulled out his phone. "I'll have my officers take a look at the footage while they're at your house."

Jake turned to Haley. "Why don't you call a locksmith right now? I don't want you staying at the house tonight unless the locks have been changed."

Haley pulled out her phone and started Googling. "I won't

cancel tomorrow's appointment until the job's done, just in case."

Detective Tillet ended his call and set his phone down on the armrest of his chair. "My officers will get back to me as soon as they've had a chance to review the footage. Jake, did you happen to notice if any of your neighbors were at home when you pulled into your driveway?"

He rubbed his brow. "It's all a bit hazy, to be honest. I'm pretty sure Becca and Anthony were home. I heard music coming through an open window. Liz's minivan was in her driveway, but I don't know if she was home or not. I don't remember seeing any lights on in the house. She and the kids could have been out and about with Stan in his car, I suppose."

"What about Harold Moore?"

Jake shrugged. "He's always home, as far as anyone knows."

Detective Tillet's phone rang and he slid his finger across the screen and pressed it to his ear. "Yeah?" The frown on his forehead deepened. "Yeah, okay. Good work. Keep me posted." He ended the call and looked up, his gaze locking with Haley's. "They were able to retrieve the footage. Your intruder was a man in a black ski mask, roughly six foot in height. Just as you feared, he opened your front door with a key."

19

*A*fter spending a couple of days at home recuperating, Jake insisted on going back to work, seemingly with no lingering side effects from the attack. Detective Tillet and his team had turned up no leads on the mysterious man in the black ski mask, other than that he had left on foot, which suggested he knew all about the newly installed cameras and had intentionally parked his vehicle out of range. It all jived with everything Haley had suspected for some time now—that her stalker had access to intimate details of her life and was well-versed in her comings and goings. It reignited her suspicions about her neighbors in the cul-de-sac. The approximate height of the intruder seemed to rule Harold out. Jim certainly had plenty of time at his disposal to conduct a campaign of terror, especially considering, by his own admission, he barely slept. And he was a hunter and a handyman, both useful skills for an intruder. Stan was a little over six foot tall, and he might have kept a key to her property after showing it, but what would be his motive for terrorizing her? And then there was Anthony, maybe the stalking was his version of acting out some sick game he played online obsessively.

The new locks gave Haley some assurance that the stalker could no longer enter her house freely, but Detective Tillet cautioned her to be doubly on guard when she was out and about, particularly getting into her car when she was alone, or after dark. He warned that the stalker might become enraged once he realized the locks had been changed and attempt a more brazen strike.

But as it turned out, the next attack came in a different form entirely. Haley was at her desk at work the following Monday when her smart phone pinged with a Facebook message. She reached for her phone, opened up the Messenger app and glanced idly at the snippet that was visible. An unfamiliar number. Frowning, she clicked on the message and scanned through it, her chest tightening as the words sank in.

You think you got away with it, don't you?

Gasping out loud, she clapped a hand over her mouth. Her thoughts careened around inside her head as she reread the words. It could mean only one thing—the dark secret that still haunted her all these years later. She cast a quick glance around the office, half-afraid someone might have noticed her horrified reaction, but the other paralegals were all engrossed in their work. As if sensing Haley's eyes on her, Natalie looked up and glanced in her direction. She raised her brows questioningly, some sixth sense telling her something was amiss.

Haley's heart hammered a frenzied rhythm as she tried to pull herself together. What had happened with Emma was the only part of her past she couldn't tell Natalie about. She and her quad sisters had promised never to speak of it to anyone again, and for good reason. Hastily, she closed up her Messenger app and slipped her phone back into her purse.

Pasting on a smile, she got to her feet and headed to the bathroom.

Once inside, she locked herself in a stall and pressed her back to the door, forcing herself to take slow, steady breaths, terrified she would succumb to the full-blown panic attack that lately seemed only ever a heartbeat away. She was clinging to the edge of the cliff of sanity with her fingernails. One of these days she might lose her grip and collapse in a blubbering heap, exposed to the world for who she really was. She took a few more deep breaths to calm herself, and then dug around in her purse for her phone. Her fingers shook so hard she almost dropped it on the tile floor. Opening up the Messenger app again, she prayed she'd only imagined the message, but the words loomed up at her, taunting, condemning, a hangman's noose of letters that spelled out what she'd done.

Sweating profusely, she drew her fingers across her brow trying to figure out what it meant, and what to do about it. Was it a threat of some kind? Was her past finally catching up with her? Apparently, someone knew what she'd done, but what did they want from her? Were they getting some sick satisfaction from tormenting her? Or were they intending to blackmail her? Tearing off a wad of toilet paper she blotted the sweat from her forehead, trying not to mess up her foundation in the process. She had to clear her head and think through the situation logically. It was possible the message wasn't connected to what had happened to Emma—her paranoia could be getting the best of her again. Maybe it was even a random message meant for someone else. After all, she hadn't recognized the sender's number. It might have landed in her inbox by mistake.

She scratched her scalp nervously. How could anyone have found out about what she'd done back in high school after all this time? No one else knew—other than her quad sisters. And it didn't make sense that any of them would send her a threatening message. They'd been in on what happened and were equally culpable. They wanted it to go away as much as she did.

Haley gritted her teeth. She needed to pull herself together before she went back out to the office. She would work this out later. There was probably some way to track where the message originated. Jake might know how to do it, but she couldn't drag him into this. She still couldn't bring herself to tell him what she'd done. It would devastate him. She would have to get to the bottom of this on her own initiative. Her mind made up, she fished around in her purse for her lip gloss and applied a generous layer, then pulled her shoulders back in an effort to bolster her courage. Before she had a chance to exit the stall, the door to the bathroom opened and whooshed shut again.

"Hales?" Natalie called out in a tentative tone. "Are you in here?"

Haley closed her eyes and grimaced. "Yeah, I'm here." She flushed the toilet and opened the stall, willing her expression to a bland neutral.

"Are you okay? You're white as a ghost." Natalie laid a concerned hand on Haley's arm as if afraid she was about to keel over.

"I'm fine." Haley slathered on a smile. "Just felt a little nauseous there for a minute or two."

Natalie's jaw dropped. "Seriously? You're not ... pregnant, are you?"

Haley gave a hollow laugh. "No, of course not. Probably something I ate."

Natalie looked unconvinced. "Are you sure that's all it is? You don't seem yourself at all."

Haley bent over the sink and made a show of washing her hands. She couldn't meet Natalie's honest gaze. The lies from her past festered inside her like a cancer. That was the problem with lies. Once you told them, they never really died, and they definitely didn't make things better. You had to cater to them, embellish them, tart them up on occasion, but you could never ignore them in the vain hope they would eventually go away. They lived on inside you like a parasite eating at you. A dormant volcano, waiting for their cover to be blown.

She hated lying to Natalie—it was slowly driving a wedge between them. Natalie was too good a friend to deceive, but she wouldn't understand how anyone could have carried out something as despicable as what the quads had done. Haley couldn't face the shame of telling her friend the truth and seeing the shock and revulsion in her eyes as it dawned on her that Haley wasn't the halfway decent person she purported to be.

She turned off the faucet and shook her hands into the sink. "I feel much better. The nausea has passed."

Natalie shrugged, looking unconvinced as she exited the bathroom.

Back at her desk, Haley dove into her work with renewed gusto, refusing to dwell on the unsettling Facebook message. She couldn't allow herself to become an emotional wreck and buckle under her workload. Nick had already expressed enough concern about her backlog, and she needed to prove she was every bit the worker he thought he'd hired.

Her phone pinged again with a message as she was packing up for the day. She flinched, as though an arrow had struck her, then bent her head and made a show of tidying up her desk, even though her thoughts had instantly scattered. Her heartbeat resounded like a gong inside her chest. She would have to wait until she reached the privacy of her car before checking the message. She couldn't risk Natalie catching her and convincing her to divulge what was wrong.

"See you tomorrow, Nats," Haley chirped, trying to nail a carefree tone. Instead, her voice sounded thin and unsure of itself.

"Hold on a minute. I'll walk out to the car with you," Natalie responded, her eyes sweeping Haley's face like a scanner reading a bar code.

Haley briefly considered telling her she had an appointment and needed to take off right away, but she didn't have the stomach for even an innocuous lie. Instead, she loitered by the door, trying not to appear as though she was falling apart inside, the message on her phone burning a hole in her purse.

"Okay, I'm all set," Natalie announced, walking over.

Together, they made their way down to the parking structure, Natalie chattering blithely about her day and a new case her boss had given her to research. Once the elevator doors opened, she turned to Haley. "Look, I know there's something you're not telling me. I'm not going to keep pressing the issue, but if you want to talk about it, I want you to know I'm here for you. And if it's something to do with the stalker, you need to call Detective Tillet ASAP. It's not safe to keep secrets now that you know for sure someone's trying to kill you."

"Yeah, you're right," Haley replied with a tight smile. "Believe me, I'm doing everything I can to protect myself. Why do you think I signed up for those self-defense classes?"

Natalie sighed. "I agree with Haruki that you're underestimating how dangerous the situation is. You should be taking lessons at the gun range."

"I couldn't shoot anyone," Haley said, her stomach heaving at the thought. She already had Emma's death on her conscience. She'd never be able to take a life, not even in self-defense.

"Just seeing a gun in your hand might be enough to send a

stalker running," Natalie pointed out. "Think about it." She beeped her car open and waved. "See you tomorrow."

Haley unlocked her car and climbed in. She waited until Natalie exited the parking lot and then pulled out her phone and jabbed at it with shaking fingers until the app opened. Another message from the same sender popped up. The words blurred in front of her as tears stung her eyes.

You're going to pay for what you did. It's only just begun.

Her shoulders shook uncontrollably as she gripped the steering wheel. These weren't messages that had gone astray in cyberspace. She was the intended recipient, and she knew with growing certainty what they alluded to. But who had sent them? A tiny moan escaped her lips as a frightening thought hit her. It was the only logical explanation. One of the quad sisters must have broken their vow of silence and confessed to someone. The dirty secret they had tried to bury was a secret no longer.

*H*aley scrunched her eyes shut, trying to stop the involuntary trembling that had spread to every part of her body. If one of the other quad sisters had told someone what they'd done that day, it was only a matter of time before it all caught up with her, before the police came knocking on her door—and not to help her. She had more to fear now than a stalker. Everything was at stake—her job, her reputation, even her marriage.

A rap on the passenger side window startled her almost out of her skin and she let out a small shriek. Jerking her head sideways, she spotted Lance peering in at her, his thatched brows drawn together over inquiring eyes.

She hastily stuffed her phone into her purse and rolled down the window.

"If you're having car trouble again, I might be able to help," Lance said, his delivery flat and unemotional, as always.

"Thanks, Lance, but everything's fine," Haley assured him, her voice teetering on the edge of control.

His nose twitched as though sniffing out the lie. "You're crying," he observed.

"I ... I just got some bad news," Haley stuttered, turning the key in ignition. "I needed a moment. I'll be all right."

Lance took a step back from the car, a befuddled expression on his face, as she reversed out of her parking spot and drove up the ramp to exit the garage.

Grimacing, she pulled out into the evening traffic. She hadn't fooled Lance any more than she'd fooled Natalie. She needed to take control of this situation before everything fell apart and her whole life caved in. She couldn't count on Detective Tillet to help her with this any longer, not now that she knew what it was about, and she wasn't going to ask Jake to trace the messages either. It was far too risky. She would have to resolve things on her own.

The first thing she had to do was figure out who was behind the messages. And that meant resurrecting the ghosts of her past. One of her quad sisters had squealed—overwhelmed by guilt, or divulged in a moment of weakness. It was time to track them down. Perhaps some of the other quads had been receiving threatening messages too. Maybe the stalker was targeting all of them. There was no telling where it would all end—blackmail seemed a likely goal.

Whatever the case, she had to get to the bottom of things, and she needed to do it swiftly and discreetly. She couldn't afford to waste another minute. Her best option was to hire a private investigator.

Her mind made up, she pulled into a Target parking lot, turned off the engine, and began Googling PI's and checking out their websites. Some appeared to be more focused on technology and internet security, and she quickly dismissed those. One site, in particular, caught her attention with its slogan, "the truth is out there, and I can find it for you," boldly plastered across the banner at the top of the page. In the text beneath, it promised personalized, discreet service, twenty-four hours a day. A one-person outfit. Exactly what she needed. She punched in the number and gripped her phone tightly to her ear.

"Fischer Investigative Services, PI Fischer speaking."

"Hi, my name's Haley—" Her voice trailed off. She hadn't thought this through properly. Should she give her last name? There wasn't much point in trying to hide it. If the PI was any good at his job, he would soon find out the names of everyone in the quad squad, including hers.

"How can I help you, Haley?" PI Fischer's tone was infused with equal measures of patience and assertiveness. No doubt he was accustomed to encouraging hesitant clients to talk.

"I was hoping you could help me track down some former friends of mine from high school."

"Sure. Would you like to make an appointment to come in and kickstart the process?"

"Is there any chance I could come by now?"

After a brief pause, PI Fischer responded, "Works for me." He rattled off an address and directions before hanging up.

Haley plugged the details into her GPS and started up the car. Hopefully, the appointment wouldn't take too long, and she could still beat Jake home. She didn't want to arouse his suspicions that she was hiding something from him. If he got wind of what she was up to, he would demand answers, and she wasn't prepared to confess everything to him and jeopardize the life she'd built with him.

As she drove, she went over in her mind exactly what she would say to the investigator. Keeping it simple was probably the best approach—sticking to her story that she wanted to reconnect with some old friends she'd lost contact with. With any luck, he wouldn't dig any deeper than necessary to root out her quad sisters' current contact details. And even if he did stumble across the story and connect her to it, she could count on his discretion. His livelihood depended on it.

PI Fischer's office was surprisingly small, tucked away above a strip mall—clean, minimalist and well-organized. The desk sported only a MacBook Pro and a leather pen holder with a handful of pens, a single highlighter and a pair of scissors.

He stood and shook hands with Haley before gesturing for her to take a seat opposite him.

"I'm glad I caught you this late," she began. "I can't imagine you actually work twenty-four hours like your website claims."

He stretched his lips into a polite smile, his hands interlaced in front of him on the desk. "I'm available twenty-four hours a day if that's what it takes. Why don't you tell me a little more about these friends of yours you want me to track down?"

"We were very close in high school," Haley explained. "But we all went our separate ways when we moved out of the area, ended up drifting apart like so often happens. I'd like to try and reconnect with them before we all turn thirty. We always used to celebrate our birthdays together."

"Do you have any contact with them on social media—Facebook or anything?"

Haley shook her head. "No. Like I said, we lost touch, and we haven't tried to make contact since. I ... don't have a Facebook account." She twiddled with her fingers, knowing he would find it odd, but they'd all agreed at the time that it would be best if there was nothing linking them with each other.

PI Fischer angled a brow. "Have you tried contacting any of their parents who are still in the area?"

Haley shifted uncomfortably in her seat. "I think most of

them retired and moved away. In any case, I'd prefer to reconnect directly with my friends."

PI Fischer gave a knowing nod, his piercing eyes evaluating her. She knew exactly what he was thinking—that there had to be a good reason she didn't want to contact the other women's parents. But she wasn't about to satisfy his curiosity. It was irrelevant to the job she was hiring him to do.

"Fair enough," he said, his tone switching to businesslike and brisk. "I'm going to need your friends' first names, last known addresses, and physical descriptions. If you have any photographs, they would be helpful too." He slid a list of questions across the desk to her. "And if you happen to know their social security numbers or birthdays, even better."

Haley reached for a pen from the black, leather holder on the desk and got to work. "How will you go about tracking them down?"

"It shouldn't be too hard," he said. "It's not like hunting down criminals on the run. Most of the time I can handle a straightforward request like yours online. I have lots of in-house resources, and I also subscribe to several proprietary databases that provide me with the kind of basic information you're looking for. I assume you want a physical address and phone number. What about an email?"

"Yes, if possible," Haley replied. "It might be easier to send them a quick email first to see if they're even interested in reconnecting."

She finished filling out the form and then handed over her credit card for PI Fischer to process an initial payment. "How long do you think it will take before you can get the information together?"

"A day or two at most." He wiggled his brows. "Just be prepared that this may not turn out the way you're hoping it will. I've been doing this a long time, and trust me when I say, you'd be amazed where some of your high school friends end up—halfway around the world, dead and buried, or doing time."

Haley gave a tight smile, her stomach knotting at the throwaway comment that hit home. They *should* be doing time—*she* should be doing time. "Let's hope for the best," she said as she got to her feet.

LESS THAN FORTY-EIGHT HOURS LATER, Haley was curled up on her couch with her laptop balanced on the armrest next to her when an email notification from PI Fischer slid across her screen. Jake was seated to her left, engrossed in a documentary about the future of technology.

Haley snapped her laptop closed with an elaborate yawn and got to her feet. "I think I'll turn in. I need to go in to the office early tomorrow."

"Okay, night, sweetheart," Jake said, scarcely glancing up from the television as she pecked him on the cheek.

She climbed the stairs to their bedroom, sank down on the bed and opened up the email from PI Fischer. After scanning the contents, she pored over the information for several more minutes. It was more detailed than she'd expected. Despite his cautionary tales, it appeared that none of her quad sisters was doing time or six feet under. All three had married, and Tina and Vivian each had a child. Lachlan was a radiologist and married to a lawyer in Los Angeles, and, judging by the zip code she lived in, she and her husband were doing extremely well for themselves.

Haley wet her lips as she clicked on the first contact. She would email each of them separately. Once she'd determined which of them had betrayed their vow of silence, she would decide what to do about it.

*H*aley's fingers moved over the keyboard, hesitantly, at first, and then faster, whipping out the message she'd rehearsed in her mind multiple times already.

Hey Viv,

It's Haley. I know you never expected to hear from me again, but something critical has surfaced. In case you're wondering, I hired a private investigator to track you down. I'm not going to beat around the bush. Someone has been talking. I've been getting Facebook messages from a stranger—threatening messages alluding to what happened. You know what I'm referring to. Whoever this person is, they know something. They've been stalking me and harassing me, telling me I'm going to pay. My tires were slashed, and a box of rotten fruit was delivered to my house. They're trying to intimidate me—maybe even kill me. They cut my brake line recently and broke in to my house and beat up my husband. I need to know if you told anyone, or even dropped a hint to anyone. I have to put an end to all this before it goes any further, and I have to do it quickly. My life's in danger. Please email me or call me as soon as you get this. My number is (916) 323-0791.

Hx4ever

HALEY LET OUT A SLOW BREATH, staring at the quad squad's secret signature that she hadn't used since her sophomore year in high school. She swallowed back the trepidation oozing its way up her throat. She was about to delve back into a world she dreaded revisiting, but there was no other way to resolve this. Before she could change her mind, she saved the message to her drafts folder and made a copy each for Lachlan and Tina. When she was done, she sank back against her pillows, reading and rereading what she had written, questioning what she was about to do, and trying to picture her quad sisters' reactions. All of a sudden, she heard Jake's footsteps coming up the stairs. Before she could talk herself out of it, she clicked send on the messages, then slammed the lid closed on her laptop and stuffed it under her side of the bed. She wriggled under the duvet and closed her eyes, feigning sleep when Jake came into the room.

He made his way to the bathroom and she listened to the whirring of his electric toothbrush, followed by the sound of the toilet flushing. When he climbed into bed, he fluffed up his pillow before flopping down on his side with a weary grunt. Minutes later, his gentle snores filled the room. Haley's eyes popped open. She rolled onto her back and stared up at the shadowy ceiling. When she was sure Jake had sunk into a deep sleep, she quietly turned back the duvet, slipped out of bed and reached for her laptop. She wasn't going to be able to sleep anyway, and she wasn't about to resort to the sleeping pills again under any circumstances. She might as well wait up in the kitchen for a bit on the off chance any of the quads responded to her email tonight.

Fingers wrapped around a freshly brewed cup of chamomile tea, Haley scrolled aimlessly through Instagram, checking out mundane pet posts and humorous memes, willing herself to calm down enough to sleep. Every so often Katniss lifted her head from her paws and peered over at her, as if questioning what she was doing up this late. After checking her email for the umpteenth time, Haley let out a frustrated sigh. No one was going to respond tonight. Even if the other quads had read her email, they'd probably take some time to think it over before deciding whether to reply or ignore her.

Just as her eyes began to grow drowsy and she'd resigned herself to turning in for the night, a notification zipped across her screen. She pulled a few shaky breaths together. *Lachlan.* With trembling fingers, she opened up her Gmail and clicked on the message.

H,

I don't know what you think you're playing at, but if this is some kind of attempt to intimidate or threaten me, make no mistake I will take legal action. My husband is a well-connected attorney and he won't hesitate to take any action he deems necessary to silence you. We agreed not to contact each other again. We were bound by oath never to speak of what happened, and I can assure you I haven't as much as hinted at it to anyone in the intervening years. Whatever kind of mess you've got yourself into, you're on your own. Consider this your final warning to serve as notice of unwarranted harassment. Your attempts to connect with me are unwanted and unwelcome. Leave me and my family alone or you'll regret it.

L

. . .

HALEY REREAD the email in a daze. It had obviously been fired off in anger—a quicker response than she'd anticipated, certainly not the one she'd been hoping for. Lachlan had made it very clear that she had no desire to involve herself in what was happening, nor had she expressed any shock or curiosity at the fact that someone knew about what they'd done. Haley groaned inwardly. Maybe Lachlan really believed she was only trying to stir things up. At least she'd confirmed that she'd kept her lips sealed all these years. Haley had no choice but to take her word for it, and wait for the other quads to respond. She shut down her laptop and stared morosely at the black screen for a long while, before getting to her feet. By the time she finally retired to bed, it was after two in the morning.

She woke with a start the next day and peered anxiously at the wall, certain there was something important she was supposed to jump on right away, but her mind was too sluggish with sleep to recall what it was. Jake was already up, and she could hear the shower running in the adjoining bathroom. Tossing the duvet aside, she swung her legs over the edge of the bed and sat up. As soon as her feet touched the floor, the emails she'd sent to her quad sisters flashed to mind. A shiver of anticipation ran down her spine. She belted her robe around her and hurried downstairs.

After letting Katniss out into the back yard, she placed an oversized mug beneath the Keurig, welcoming the tantalizing aroma of fresh coffee. She carried her mug and laptop over to the kitchen table and opened up her Gmail, holding her breath as she went through the emails in her inbox. She hit refresh several times, but to her dismay no responses from the other quads popped up. Either they hadn't checked their email yet, or they were reeling from the shock of hearing from her after all these years and debating what to do about it. Haley slammed her laptop shut in frustration and took her coffee upstairs to shower and dress for work.

As the morning progressed, she struggled to keep her focus and finish the work Nick had earmarked as priority.

"Something bothering you?" Natalie asked, pausing briefly at Haley's desk on her way to the staff lounge.

Haley smiled weakly. "Just a rough night. I couldn't sleep. Another shot of coffee will get me through."

Natalie gave a disparaging snort. "It's me you're talking to. I know something's up, but if you don't want to chat, that's your call. Just don't tell me everything's okay when evidently it isn't. I'm getting tired of being lied to."

Natalie strode off before Haley could respond. She twisted the ends of her hair nervously, shocked at the tone Natalie had taken with her. The last thing she wanted to do was alienate the one true friend she'd made here, but she was pushing Natalie further and further away by her ongoing evasiveness. Her past felt as though it was encroaching like a mountainous wall of water—a tsunami threatening to bury her in the debris of her lies.

When lunch rolled around, Haley grabbed her car keys and marched out of the office with a determined air, praying Natalie wouldn't intercept her.

In the parking garage, Lance gave her a discreet nod from the dumpster where he was busy emptying trash. An involuntary shiver crossed her shoulders as she strode toward her car. Despite having written him off as harmless, it bothered her that he often seemed to be working down here when she was leaving. She was about to turn the key in the ignition when a thought occurred to her. Was it possible he was spying on her for someone else? If that was the case, maybe she could sweet talk him into divulging who had put him up to it. She left her purse lying on the passenger seat and walked hesitantly over to him, chewing on her lip.

His eyes twitched in her direction as she approached. He stopped tossing garbage bags into the dumpster and plunged his hands awkwardly into his pockets. "Everything all right?" he asked, jerking his chin at her car.

Haley stretched a pitiful smile across her face. "Yes, thanks, Lance. My car's fine. But I wanted to ask you something. I figured you might know the answer as you seem to spend a lot of time down here."

He rubbed a hand dubiously across his jaw. "Oh?"

Haley furrowed her brow and then lowered her voice to a tremulous whisper. "Have you by chance noticed anyone watching me? Hanging around in the shadows, or by my car, anything suspicious like that?"

Lance scratched his scalp for several minutes, staring at his feet. When he looked up again, his eyes were filled with concern. "Is someone bothering you? 'Cause if they are, you should report them."

Haley heaved her shoulders up and down in dramatic fashion. "That's just it, I don't know who it is, otherwise I would have reported them already. Someone's been sending me threatening messages on social media. And I have the feeling they've been following me." She wrapped her arms around herself and waited for Lance to respond.

He shuffled his feet nervously. "Can't say I've seen anyone hanging about. And I've been keeping an eye on things down here ever since your tire was slashed." He jerked his chin up at the cameras protruding from the corners of the parking garage. "They won't get away with it now that the cameras are working again."

Haley smiled gratefully. "You're right. That makes me feel better. Thank you, Lance. I'm sorry to have bothered you."

He nodded solemnly, then turned to haul another garbage bag from his trash cart and toss it into the dumpster. Haley walked back to her car and started it up with a resigned sigh.

Lance wasn't savvy enough to be duplicitous. She was fairly certain he wasn't spying on her on anyone's behalf—he was only doing his job, and he was very conscientious about it. It was time she separated her paranoia from the real threat, or she'd never get to the bottom of things.

She pulled out of the parking garage and drove to a quiet coffee shop on a side street where she was unlikely to run into any of her colleagues. Her stomach wasn't up to holding down a full lunch, but she could use a caffeine and sugar rush to fight her exhaustion. Armed with a mocha and a carrot and pumpkin seed muffin, she wound her way to a small table tucked in the back corner of the cafe. She lifted her steaming drink to her lips and began scrolling through her messages and emails. Sucking in a breath, she set the paper cup back down on the table, untouched.

Vivian had responded.

H,

I got your email. My skin's been crawling ever since. I can't believe what's been happening to you. Trust me, I haven't breathed a word to anyone all these years. I wouldn't have dared to after what we went through. I haven't received any messages or threats yet, but I'm afraid I might be next. If they found out about you, then they know about all of us. I still can't forgive myself for what we did. My high-school self haunts me to this day. I just keep rereading your email in disbelief. I have a three-year-old son now —Alex. I hope I haven't put him in any danger. My husband doesn't know about what happened. I haven't had any contact with Lachlan or Tina since high school, but I can't picture either of them saying anything. We swore on our lives we wouldn't. What are we going to do? I'm so scared. How are we going to find out who this person is? And what if there's more than one of them? If they go to the police, we're screwed. Our lives are over. Even if they don't prosecute us, the scandal would ruin our lives, not to mention my husband's dental practice. Email me back and let me know what you find out as soon as you hear from the others.

Vx 4ever

HALEY STARED at the signature that had once ignited such a feeling of belonging inside her, and now denoted guilt by association. Vivian's reaction had been on the opposite end of the spectrum to Lachlan's, but the gist of her response was the same—she'd told no one about what happened. That left Tina—who had yet to reply. And perhaps she never would. After all, if she'd been the one who'd let slip their secret, it was unlikely she'd be willing to come clean and admit it without some pressure being put on her.

Haley tapped her fingernails impatiently on the table, debating her next move. The customer at the adjacent table looked up from his book and threw her an irritated look. She grimaced an apology as she reached for her mocha. She would give Tina until the end of the day to respond. After that, she would pick up the phone and call the number PI Fischer had dug up. One way or another, she would hunt down the creep who was destroying her life, and put an end to his campaign of terror before he struck again.

---

*A*t five o'clock, Haley began packing up her desk, her stomach churning with apprehension. Tina still hadn't responded to her email. There was nothing else for it but to take the initiative and call her. But she couldn't wait until she went home in case Jake was already back from work. She would have to look for a quiet spot to pull over somewhere along the way.

From her desk, Natalie threw Haley a reproachful look before swinging her purse over her shoulder and getting to her feet. As she strode to the door, she made a point of bantering with the other paralegals. It pained Haley to see the wedge her deception had driven between them, but she couldn't deal with Natalie's righteous indignation at the moment. She was too embroiled in monsters from her past. She couldn't allow her old life to cross paths with the new one she'd worked so hard to build—and, at all costs, she couldn't risk losing Jake.

Haley chewed on her lip as she drove to a small park a short distance from Huntington and Dodd. She pulled up next to a children's play area and switched off the engine. For several minutes, she watched a succession of rosy-cheeked toddlers trundling up ladders and slithering down slides, limbs askew, before mustering up the courage to pull out her phone and dial Tina's number. It rang a couple of times and, just as she'd resigned herself to leaving a voicemail, a wary voice said, "Hello?"

"Tina, it's me, Haley." She swallowed down the trepidation rising in her chest before plowing on in a breathless tone. "Did you get my email?"

After a ponderous silence, Tina answered in a guarded tone, "You shouldn't have contacted me. Did you email the others too?"

Haley debated with herself before responding. She didn't want to give out too much information up front, not before she'd heard what Tina had to say for herself. "We can talk about the others in a minute. First, I need to know if you told anyone what happened. And don't lie to me. My life's been an absolute nightmare for the past few months. Someone knows, Tina. And they've got it in for me. They tried to kill me."

When Tina spoke again, the words came out in a strained whisper. "Do you ... have kids?"

Haley gripped her phone tighter, the palpable note of fear in Tina's voice ratcheting up her own dread of what was coming next. "No, but I know you have a daughter. If someone found out what we did, then all of our families are at risk. If this comes out, the media will destroy our lives, you know that as well as I do. You need to tell me the truth, Tina. I can't do anything about it if you don't come clean."

"That's assuming it was me," Tina said defensively. "You can't prove anything."

Fear coiled in Haley's gut. It sounded like an admission of sorts that Tina had ratted them out. Haley would have to tread carefully to extract the truth from her.

"I'm not assuming it was you," she replied. "I'm simply asking you to tell me if you know anything at all about what's been happening to me. We swore an oath to protect each other by keeping our mouths shut. You owe me the truth at least. We have to stop this person from talking and hurting our families. And if we need to come together one last time to do that, so be it."

Tina let out a sharp breath. "How are we going to stop them?"

Haley gritted her teeth in frustration. She still hadn't got a straight answer. Tina was deliberately dancing around the issue, but Haley was fairly certain she'd told someone, or perhaps inadvertently let their secret slip. "I have a few ideas," Haley replied with more confidence than she felt. "It depends on who this person is, and how they react when we confront them."

In reality, Haley had no clue how she was going to confront her stalker, once she identified him. It was probably a matter the police were better equipped to handle, but she didn't dare involve them anymore than she already had. She still wasn't sure what the stalker's motivation was. It seemed more and more likely that it was someone from school who had an axe to grind with her and the other quads. They'd rubbed a lot of people the wrong way back then. It was entirely possible someone still harbored a grudge and had been only too thrilled to find out their dark secret and use it against them. Haley wracked her brains trying to think of who Tina might have blabbed to, but no one came to mind as a likely candidate.

"Do you think this person would hurt our families?" Tina asked, her voice wobbling.

"I don't doubt it for one minute. They've already hurt my family," Haley reminded her. "They beat up my husband. What if your husband's next, how are you going to feel about that if you keep your mouth shut when you could have done something to stop it?"

"You don't think they would hurt my daughter, do you?" A hint of desperation had crept into Tina's voice.

Haley steeled herself. She wasn't about to reassure Tina that her kid wasn't in any danger. It might be the very motivation she needed to finally start talking.

"I don't know what they're capable of," Haley responded. "They cut my brake line so that should tell you something." She studied her nails trying to resist the urge to scream down the phone at Tina and demand that she tell her what she'd done. Tina had always been one to process things slowly. She was likely mulling over her options even now, weighing the consequences of coming clean. If she had talked to someone, it wouldn't have been something she'd done lightly, or divulged in a drunken state. Tina was far too circumspect for that. There must have been a good reason for it, although Haley couldn't think of one that justified breaking their oath to one another.

Growing desperate at the protracted silence on the other end of the line, she opted to ratchet up the pressure. "Please, Tina. I'm begging you. I'm afraid for my life at this point. I can't sleep or eat, my work's suffering, my marriage is cracking under the strain. Just tell me the truth, that's all I'm asking you to do."

"Promise ... you won't say anything to the other quads." Tina's voice sounded small, almost as if it had traveled from some distant planet or other time zone.

Haley dug her fingernails deep into her palms willing herself to stay calm and not rush her. "I swear it will stay between us. Viv and Lachlan haven't received any threatening messages, so they don't need to know anything. Whoever's behind this is only targeting me, for now."

Tina exhaled wearily. "I didn't mean to say anything. I was only trying to show a little compassion, and … it slipped out."

Haley frowned. Compassion was hardly an excuse for breaking their oath, but she needed to tread gently now that Tina was talking at last. "Okay, tell me exactly how it went down."

"It was about five years ago. I was dating this guy before I met my husband. One night we went out for drinks and he started telling me all about how his mother hanged herself when he was only fifteen. He broke down and began crying in my arms. I didn't know what to say. I was trying to comfort him. I mentioned that a girl in our school had hung herself and that I understood how shocking it must have been for him."

"That's all you said?" Haley demanded impatiently. "You didn't tell him what we did?"

"Well … not exactly," Tina replied, sounding decidedly uncomfortable.

"Not *exactly*," Haley echoed, unable to curb her mounting frustration any longer. "What's that supposed to mean?"

"I told him one of my friends had posted something on a notice board that upset and embarrassed the girl and that I felt responsible for not stepping in and stopping it from happening. That's it, I swear, Hales. I didn't mention names or anything."

Haley grimaced. "Where did you meet this guy? Was he from Chino Hills?"

"No, I met him while I was working in San Francisco. But he said he had friends in Chino Hills. He knew our high school."

Haley scrunched her eyes shut. "What was his name?"

"Travis. Travis Ramsey."

"I need to talk to him. Do you still have his contact information?"

"I might have his cell phone number. But I've no idea where he's living anymore. He moved out of the area after we broke up."

"I can track him down. Just give me whatever information you have for him."

"Please don't mention my name," Tina begged.

"Of course not. I'm not going to confront him directly. I'll have the investigator I hired look into him, try to find out if he's behind what's been going on. Don't worry, there's no way he can trace anything back to you."

"I still don't understand why he's harassing you," Tina said.

"It might not be him," Haley pointed out. "He could have talked to someone at our high school who had an axe to grind with us."

"There's no shortage of people who have every right to hate us," Tina said sounding chagrined. "I'm really sorry, Hales. Like I said, I never intended to say anything. It just happened in the moment—he was so distraught."

Haley pressed her lips together tightly in disapproval. She wasn't prepared to serve up platitudes to ease Tina's conscience. What she'd done was a blatant betrayal of their oath. But Haley wasn't that same vengeful quad sister she'd been back in high school, and she didn't have any desire to drag this out any further. What she needed to do now was focus on damage control.

"My husband just walked in," Tina hissed into the phone. "I have to go. I'll text you that number." The line went dead before Haley had a chance to respond.

Dropping her phone into her lap, she draped her arms over the steering wheel and squeezed her eyes shut. The nightmare she'd lived with all these years had finally reared its ugly head back up to haunt her. Of all the rotten luck that, in a moment of alcohol-induced empathy, Tina had spilled their dirty, little secret to some guy with friends in Chino Hills—friends who might even have gone to their high school for all she knew.

Haley straightened up and stared out at the murky playground, a tangle of iron frames and plastic tubes, now steeped in shadows. The herd of chubby-legged children had thinned out, headed home with their parents to begin their evening routines.

She reached for her phone again and opened up her notes app. Resigning herself to resurrecting the unwelcome ghosts of her past, she hit the speaker button and began dictating a list of classmates from Chino Hills High who had every reason to harbor a grudge deep enough to murder for.

23

*F*or the second night in a row, Haley barely slept. She had confirmation now that their secret was out, and there was no telling how far it had spread. It might be only a matter of time before her stalker called in an anonymous tip to the press, or even the police. What kind of a sick, twisted person would do this to her? She'd made an awful mistake, but she'd turned her life around because of it. Surely, she didn't deserve what was happening to her now.

Haley stumbled through the rest of the day in a daze, and her work suffered as a result. Nick called her into his office and chewed her up about several errors he'd uncovered in the research she'd turned in to him. Chastened, she took her case notes back to her desk to make the requisite corrections. She could feel Natalie's eyes on her as she worked, but she avoided looking in her direction. They were scheduled for their next self-defense class after work that evening, but Haley was beginning to wish she hadn't involved Natalie in her mess. It only obligated her to keep answering questions she couldn't answer honestly without revealing the ugly truth.

When the day drew to a close, Natalie approached her with a sheepish grin. "Do you want to ride together?" Her tone was conciliatory, edged with caution. "It's tough to find a parking spot at the studio."

Haley shrugged. "Sure, I guess." In all honesty, she'd rather be free to jump in her own car and drive straight home after class, but she had a feeling Natalie was seeking an opportunity to straighten things out between them.

In the underground parking structure, Haley retrieved her gym bag from her car before climbing into Natalie's Camry, thankful that, for once, Lance was nowhere to be seen. "I'm sorry I haven't been forthcoming about what's been going on," she offered as Natalie started up the car. "It's difficult to talk about it."

"That's kind of the point of having friends though—to help you through the tough times," Natalie replied, as she pulled out onto the road. "What concerns you should concern me. But I can't help you if you insist on keeping it to yourself."

Haley leaned her head against the side window and stared out at the cars whizzing by. "It's just that I think what's been happening has something to do with my past—my high school years to be exact—and I was hoping not to involve you in it. I just want to forget that stage of my life. I wasn't a happy person back then. I didn't know who I was, and I did a lot of things I'm ashamed of now."

Natalie let out a snort. "None of us knew who we were in high school. That's why it's called *growing up*."

Haley nodded pensively. "But some of us make mistakes that follow us for the rest of our lives."

Natalie pulled her brows together. "How big a mistake are we talking here? Did you give up a kid for adoption or something?"

Haley gave a wry grin. "No, nothing like that."

"So, is your stalker some old boyfriend who's still obsessed with you?"

Haley shook her head. "No, at least he's not an old boyfriend of mine. But it's possible he dated a friend of mine."

"Well, that's progress, at least you have a suspect now. Why would he want to stalk you if he dated your friend?"

"Like I said, I wasn't the same person back then that I am today. You wouldn't have liked me in high school, Nats. I was what you would call a mean girl. I did the kinds of things that make people hold grudges against you—the kinds of things that scar a person for life."

Natalie was silent for a moment as she pulled up outside the studio and put the car into park. "We all did junk in high school. How bad are we talking?"

"Big league bad." Haley turned and met Natalie's inquiring gaze. "If you really want to know, a spiteful prank I played backfired, and a girl died as a result. No one knew I was behind it, other than three close friends who were with me at the time."

Natalie's eyes grew wide. "Yikes! What was the prank?"

Haley threw her a woebegone look. "Does it matter? It makes me sick just thinking about it. The point is, I was a complete jerk. I was part of a gang, and we spent our time tormenting socially awkward kids. There—I've said it now. That's why I didn't want to tell you about my past. It nauseates me to think about how I treated people back then. Anyway, I hired a PI to track down the other girls in my gang—there were four of us and we called ourselves the Quad Squad. I found out that one of them told an old boyfriend about what we'd done. Turns out he had friends in Chino Hills where we went to high school. Someone must have put two and two together. So, the cat's out of the bag so to speak."

Natalie grimaced. "What are you going to do about it?"

"Hire the PI to track this guy down and tail him for a bit, try and figure out if he's the one who's actually stalking me. If it's not him, I'll have to confront him and find out who he talked to at my old high school."

"This is getting really creepy," Natalie said, sounding subdued. "I think it's time you took Haruki's advice and get yourself a gun."

Haley swallowed hard. "I want to see what the PI comes up with first before I decide on my next steps." Her phone dinged signaling an incoming message and she pulled it out. Her heart skipped a beat when she saw it was from Tina. "One of the girls in my gang just sent me her ex-boyfriend's contact info. I'm going to email this to PI Fischer right away. The sooner he jumps on it, the better." She typed a quick explanatory email and hit send before climbing out of the car.

For the next hour-and-a-half, Haley and Natalie concentrated on Haruki's demonstrations of various self-defense techniques. Haley forced herself to pay close attention, only too aware that it could mean the difference between life and death if her stalker confronted her at some point in the coming days.

"Excellent work, ladies," Haruki said with a neat bow at the end of the session. His piercing eyes searched Haley's face. "I can see you're taking your training very seriously. I assume your stalker's still at large?"

Haley nodded, not trusting herself to speak.

Haruki blinked solemnly. "I stand by what I said. You can't rely on your ability to outfight someone who is stalking you. A stalker has the element of surprise on his side."

"That's what I've been trying to tell her," Natalie chimed in. "She needs a gun."

"I'm hiring a private investigator to track down the

stalker," Haley answered. "Once I know who I'm dealing with, I'll decide how far to take things. With enough evidence from the PI, the police might even be able to make an arrest."

Haruki rubbed his chin thoughtfully. "Enlisting the help of law enforcement would be wise." He bowed again by way of dismissal and stepped off the mats.

The girls thanked him and made their way out of the studio to Natalie's car.

"If you want, I can follow you home," Natalie offered when she pulled into Huntington and Dodd's parking structure. "I feel like the stalker has upped the ante of late. And Detective Tillet warned you not to go anywhere on your own after dark."

"Thanks, but it's not necessary," Haley assured her. "I'm perfectly safe in my car. I'll text you as soon as I get home."

Natalie twisted her lips to signal her disapproval. "Your choice. I'll wait until you're safely out of the parking garage at least."

Haley hugged her good-bye. "Thanks, Nats. You're a good friend for sticking by me."

A short time later, Haley pulled into her driveway without incident. The lights were on, indicating that Jake was already home, thankfully. After her conversation with Tina earlier, she was more afraid than ever of being alone. There was a long list of people from her high school days who had a bone to pick with her, and any one of them could be her stalker—she might even have more than one.

"Hey sweetheart," Jake said when she walked into the living room. "How was your exercise class?"

Haley flopped down on the couch next to him. "Exhausting."

He wrinkled his nose. "You stink. You'd better hit the shower before you snuggle up with me."

She laughed. "After I eat. I'm starving. Did you pick up anything?"

"I grabbed us some salads on the way home. Yours is in the fridge."

Haley leaned over and planted a kiss on his lips. "You're the best." She lifted her hand and stroked his cheek gently. "I'm so glad you're safe, Jake. I don't know what I'd do if anything had happened to you."

He squeezed her hand softly, his eyes clouding over. "Don't be silly. Nothing's going to happen to me, I promise. Or you, I'll make sure of it."

Haley got to her feet and made her way into the kitchen to greet Katniss. She jumped up, wagging her tail excitedly. After ruffling her ears and petting her, Haley washed her hands and retrieved her dinner from the fridge. She settled down at the kitchen table and poured dressing over the goat cheese and arugula salad. Her stomach rumbled. After all the calories she'd burned at her self-defense class, she could have used something a little more substantial than a salad to eat, but she was grateful not to have to start cooking this late at night.

She dug her fork into the lettuce and propped her phone up against the fruit bowl, searching for something mind-numbing to watch on YouTube. After devouring her salad, she hit pause on the home remodel episode she was engrossed in and went over to the refrigerator to dig out a tub of ice cream from the freezer box. She figured she'd earned the calories.

When she returned to her phone, bowl in hand, she noticed a new email from PI Fischer. Had he dug up the information she'd requested on Travis Ramsey already? She parked her spoon in her ice cream and opened up her Gmail to find out.

. . .

Hi Haley,

I got your email earlier and did a quick online search for Travis Ramsey. The phone number you gave me is no longer valid, but it wasn't too hard to track him down through social media. Interestingly enough, it appears that he's living only a few miles from you. I've enclosed a folder with some photographs which I pulled from social media. Most of them are from several years ago—I had a hard time finding more recent shots. If you need anything else, let me know. Otherwise, consider this a freebie as it only took me fifteen minutes or so to pull this together for you.

Best regards,

PI Fischer

HALEY'S BREATH baulked in her throat. Was Travis Ramsey—Tina's ex—really her stalker? The fact that he lived only a few miles away seemed to indicate he was a likely candidate. With shaking fingers, she opened the folder in the email to access the photos PI Fischer had enclosed. She clicked on the first one and stared at it in disbelief.

The face was bearded, and the forehead slightly more elongated, but the eyes looking back at her were Jake's.

24

*A*t eight o'clock the next morning, Haley found herself sitting in a chair opposite PI Fischer in his office, watching his reaction as he compared the photo of Jake she'd given him to the photos of Travis Ramsey he'd unearthed on social media. She'd taken a personal day off work, unable to face the thought of tackling the stack of case files on her desk while wrestling with the ever-evolving nightmare blowing up in her face. It had been chilling to learn that her stalker was living within a five-mile radius of her, but the fact that he looked eerily like her husband had completely unraveled what was left of her nerves. The worst alternative of all, the one she refused to dwell on, was that the man might actually be Jake, wearing a false beard to disguise himself. Maybe Edith had been right after all.

"So, do you think it's him?" she prodded, when PI Fischer leaned back in his chair and slid the photo of Jake across the desk to her.

"I'm not sure. I have to agree with you that he looks a bit like him, but that could be a fluke. Any chance he could be a relative?"

"Jake doesn't have any siblings," Haley replied, her fingers fluttering nervously to her throat.

"What about a cousin or something? Have you met any of Jake's relatives?"

Haley shook her head. She wracked her brains trying to recall if he'd ever mentioned a cousin. "Jake's parents died in a car crash a couple of years ago. His dad was an only child, and his mom's only sister never married."

"That doesn't rule out the possibility that she had a son," PI Fischer pointed out. "In fact, Jake might not even know he has a cousin."

Haley frowned. "I suppose I could ask him about it, but I don't want to alert him to the fact that I've hired an investigator."

PI Fischer nodded thoughtfully. "In that case, if you want to leave it with me, I'll do some more digging and try to find out if this Travis Ramsey is a relative of Jake's." He scratched the stubble on his chin. "You need to understand that this could change everything. I don't know if you've thought about this angle yet, but it's possible the stalker is after your husband, and not you at all. Everything he did to you might have been to get at Jake indirectly. If there was bad blood over something in the past between Jake's mom and her sister, it's possible this is someone out for revenge."

Goosebumps pricked Haley's skin as she tried to digest what PI Fischer was saying. It was a possibility she hadn't considered until now. It would certainly explain why the intruder had beaten up Jake and not her. But she didn't entirely buy the theory. The stalker had made a point of letting her know he'd found out about her terrible secret. It felt too personal to be a campaign of terror directed solely at Jake. She exhaled a shaky breath. Wherever the truth led, she was going to need help getting there. She looked across at PI Fischer and gave a reluctant nod. "Please do whatever it takes to find out if there's a connection between this man and my husband. Wherever the truth lies, I need to get to it."

PI Fischer's expression darkened. "In the meantime, you'll have to watch your back. Do you own a gun?"

"No, I hate the idea, although I'm not going to rule it out at this point. I do have a German shepherd at home, and I just started taking self-defense classes."

PI Fischer tapped his knuckles on the desk, looking contemplative. "Well, it's a start. All things considered, I'm going to advise you not to share any of what we've discussed with your husband until we clear up this man's identity. We don't know yet what transpired between them. There could be some history there that your husband may not want you dredging up. Of course, it's entirely your decision."

"I won't say anything for now." Haley reached for her purse. "Please contact me as soon as you have any more information."

"You bet," PI Fischer said. "This could take me a day or two, so bear with me."

He shook hands with her across the desk and then escorted her to the door.

Back in her car, Haley sat quietly for a few moments thinking about the photos of Travis Ramsey that PI Fischer had shown her. It was hard to deny the striking resemblance to Jake. Even PI Fischer had acknowledged it, and he was a trained investigator. But what did it mean? Part of her wanted to drive straight over to Jake's office and confront him with the photos, but of course she wouldn't do that. Like PI Fischer had said, it was possible Jake didn't even know he had a cousin. Besides, there was still a chance the resemblance between the two men was purely coincidental. She needed to be patient and wait and see what PI Fischer came up with. If Jake found out that she'd been investigating him, she would have to explain everything—including why she'd hired a PI in the first place—and then the whole sorry story of her past would come tumbling out. Jake would feel utterly betrayed once he realized she wasn't the woman he thought he'd married. It could very well spell the end of their marriage.

Haley toyed distractedly with her phone. She considered calling her parents but ultimately decided against it. She hadn't talked to them much in the past few weeks, not wanting to worry them needlessly until she got to the bottom of the stalker situation. Frowning, she tossed the phone into her purse. The thought of going home to an empty house after her conversation with PI Fischer was disconcerting. On a whim, she decided to drive over to the martial arts studio and see if Haruki was available to give her a private lesson. Maybe it would bolster her courage a little. At the very least, she could kill some time practicing the moves he'd taught her so far. The studio would be quiet this time of the morning without the after-school crowd unleashing their boundless energy.

Just as she pulled into the parking lot, her phone dinged with a new message. She turned off the ignition and glanced at the screen. *Lachlan.* Her heart began to race. What now? Surely, she wasn't going to make good on her threats to sue her.

Hey H,

I came on kind of strong in my last email, but to be honest, you completely blindsided me. I still stand by my original comments that I don't want to get embroiled in whatever is happening to you, but I need to know if either Viv or Tina admitted to talking to anyone about what happened. I've been thinking it over, and this could potentially be very serious for all of us. My husband's an experienced lawyer and, if necessary, he can handle this for us and make it all go away. But as you can imagine, I have no desire to drag him into this unnecessarily if it can be avoided. Please let me know what you hear from the others ASAP.

Lx4ever

HALEY STARED AT THE EMAIL. Unlike in her first message, Lachlan had reverted to using her quad sister signature, purely as leverage of course. It was typical of Lachlan to go after something she wanted by sweetening the pot—she hadn't changed much. She always could turn the charm on and off like a faucet. Haley closed the message and put her phone away. She wouldn't respond to the email, at least not yet. She'd given Tina her word that she wouldn't betray her confidence, and she didn't trust Lachlan not to use this against them. She only hoped PI Fischer was able to track down the information she needed quickly so she could get to the bottom of things before Lachlan's hot shot lawyer husband started meddling in the situation.

Before she could talk herself out of it, she climbed out of her car and strode into the Eagle Martial Arts studio. To her disappointment, Haruki had the day off, but she took to the mats and got to work practicing her moves, more painfully aware than ever that her life might depend on it. After an hour of sweating it out, she finally called it a day.

Half-starved after her intense workout, she drove to a tiny Vietnamese restaurant off the beaten track and parked herself at a table at the back, out of view of the windows and passersby. She was halfway through her lunch when she got a call from PI Fischer. Swallowing a mouthful of food, she pressed the phone to her ear. "Hello?"

"Hi, Haley. Hope I didn't interrupt you."

"No, I took a personal day. I can't concentrate on anything other than the stalker at this point."

"That's understandable. As a matter of fact, after you hear what I have to say, you're going to want to put all your energy into getting to the bottom of this situation you're in."

A jolt of fear went through Haley at the somber note in his voice. She set down her fork and pushed her bowl to one side. "What did you find out?"

PI Fischer cleared his throat. "It turns out Travis Ramsey is Dillon Ramsey's brother."

"Dillon Ramsey—who's that? Doesn't sound familiar." Haley frowned in frustration.

PI Fischer grunted. "I figured you'd never heard of him."

"I don't know either of them," Haley responded. "Should I?"

For a long moment there was silence on the other end of the line. "Dillon Ramsey changed his name to Jake Wilder four years ago."

2 5

---

*H*aley's throat constricted until she could barely take a breath. She clutched the phone tighter. *No!* It couldn't be true. This was worse than anything she'd envisioned. *Jake's brother was her stalker.* That meant her husband had lied to her about being an only child. But why? Her mind scrambled to put the pieces together. Did Jake know his brother was behind the stalking? She immediately banished the thought from her head. Of course, he didn't. Jake must be estranged from his brother. It was the only explanation that made sense—that's why he'd told her he didn't have any siblings. There had to be a good reason why he'd cut all ties with his brother. Maybe Travis had some kind of criminal past. He might even owe Jake money or something.

"You're probably right about there being bad blood between them," Haley said, once she'd recovered sufficiently from her shock to speak. "That would explain why Jake's brother is stalking both of us. He's trying to get at Jake through me. Were you able to find out anything at all about what transpired between them in the past? Maybe it had something to do with the inheritance after their parents died in the car crash."

Another long pause ensued before PI Fischer responded, "Haley, their father died of cancer when the boys were still in elementary school. Their mother remarried, and she and her current husband live in a retirement community called Sunrise Manor two hours north of here."

Haley's gut twisted with a new fear. She shook her head slowly as if to convince herself that what she was hearing couldn't possibly be true. "No, that isn't right. They're both dead. Jake told me all about how the accident happened. The roads were slick that day and his father took a bend too quickly. He died instantly, Jake's mother lingered on for a couple of days in the hospital."

"I don't know why he told you that," PI Fischer replied. "I can only assume it's because he's estranged from his mother and stepfather, and he didn't want you to know they were still alive. I can try and look into their relationship and find out what happened between them if you want."

Haley pressed her knuckles to her lips, frantically trying to think things through and make sense of it all. Jake had lied to her about his parents too, but there must be an explanation. Maybe his mother was crazy—just like his brother. Maybe she'd taken Jake's brother's side. Jake might be trying to protect his wife from his crazy family in the best way he knew how. But a tiny voice in her head whispered another possibility—that Jake had deceived her for some malevolent reason. She wasn't sure she could trust his motives. There was only one way to get to the bottom of it all. "Email me his mother's address," she replied firmly. "I'll drive up there and talk to her myself."

"Do you want me to come with you?" PI Fischer offered, a note of concern in his voice.

Haley considered his offer for a moment. She welcomed

the idea of someone accompanying her, but it might only hamper her search for the truth. "Thanks for the offer but if you come with me, his mother might be more reluctant to talk to me, especially if her son's in some kind of trouble with the law. I need to handle this myself, find out once and for all what's going on." She chewed the inside of her cheek as she considered the significance of what PI Fischer had unearthed. If it turned out that Jake—*a.k.a. Dillon*—and his brother, Travis, were not estranged after all, it presented the frightening possibility that Jake had colluded with his brother in this campaign of terror against her. But that didn't make any sense. Why would her husband do this to her? And why had he allowed his own brother to beat him up? Was it all in a bid to cover up the fact that they were stalking her?

Shaken to her core, Haley ended the call and plugged in the address for the assisted living facility on her phone. According to her maps app, it was a two-hour-and-eight-minute drive. That gave her barely enough time to drive there and back before Jake returned home from work around seven. As far as he knew, she'd taken a personal day for a dental appointment, and she'd promised to make his favorite dinner tonight. It would be best to postpone her visit to Sunrise Manor until the following day. There was nothing else for it, but to take another personal day and risk Nick's ire, and this time she wouldn't disclose her plans to Jake.

Resigned to her course of action, she drove to the grocery store and purchased the items she needed to make Jake's favorite pasta dish—*Dillon's* favorite dish. She still couldn't get her head around the idea that her husband's real name was Dillon Ramsey. She only hoped she didn't accidentally let the name slip over dinner. Her nerves jangled as she pushed her creaking cart toward the checkout. Somehow, she had to get through the evening without alerting Jake to the fact that she'd uncovered his web of lies.

By the time he arrived home from work, Haley had already downed a glass of wine, but it did little to calm her nerves. Thankfully, Jake was preoccupied with a deal that had landed him several new clients that day and didn't seem to notice that Haley was making little conversation. Nonetheless, she breathed out a sigh of relief when he finally disappeared into the living room to catch a football game he'd set to record earlier. When she checked on him a little later, he'd nodded off on the couch. She closed the door quietly on him and let Katniss out before sitting down at the kitchen table and scrolling through her phone. Her eyes widened when she spotted a new email from Vivian.

Hey H,

Have you heard anything back from the others yet? I think someone's been watching me too. I can't sleep anymore. I'm so frightened. I haven't been able to take my son to daycare for the past few days. I'm scared someone's going to snatch him. I can't go on like this. What are we going to do, Hales? I feel so guilty about what we did—especially now that I'm a mother myself. I knew this was going to come back to haunt us one day. I wish I'd never gone along with it. Please email me back and let me know what's going on.

Vx4Ever

HALEY GRIMACED and swiftly deleted the email as she'd done with the others. She couldn't risk Jake inadvertently coming across it. Her heartbeat thudded erratically in her chest. She wasn't going to respond to Vivian, not until she had clarity on the situation. Suddenly everything she'd believed about her stalker was up in the air. She needed to get her facts straight before she contacted the other quads again. She was still reeling from shock at the discovery that Jake had a brother—a brother who was stalking them. Some of the dots were connecting, but the biggest question playing in her mind now was whether Travis was wreaking havoc on Jake's life, or working with Jake to wreak havoc on hers. Those were two very different scenarios, and until she knew where the truth lay, she couldn't trust her own husband. She grimaced as she unlocked a file drawer and pulled out a couple of wedding photos to stash in her purse. She might need them tomorrow to convince Jake's mother and stepfather who she was.

She slept little that night, relieved when an orange glow in the sky heralded morning at last. Dressed in her workout clothes, she let Katniss out in the back yard before taking her for a quick walk around the block. When she returned, Jake was puttering around in the kitchen making breakfast. He poured her a mug of coffee and kissed her on the cheek. "Hey sweetheart. Sleep well?"

"Great," she lied with a plastic smile. "I need to jump in the shower and get going. Nick has to be in court early this morning. I'll catch up with you tonight."

She headed upstairs and closed the bathroom door behind her, trembling all over as she scrubbed at her cheek where Jake's lips had briefly rested. *Dillon's* lips. She didn't know the man she'd been living with at all. Was he a monster? Or was her husband's life in as much danger as hers from the estranged brother he'd tried in vain to cut all ties with?

After showering, Haley pulled on black slacks and a print blouse, and applied a light dusting of powder and lipstick before making her way out to her car. For the next two hours as she drove north, she played out in her mind what she would say to Jake's mother and stepfather when she finally met them. She needed to modify her presentation for every eventuality. They might have disowned their sons, cut off all contact. Or they could have dementia for all she knew. Would they be hostile or welcoming once she told them who she was? Did they know she existed? A finger of fear tingled down her spine. What if Jake's brother was following her right now? She could only assume he had to go to work at some point, so the odds were in her favor that he wasn't trailing her. At least that's what she chose to believe. The alternative was too unsettling.

Shortly before noon she pulled into the parking lot at Sunrise Manor. Gentle walkways curved around well-mani-cured, green lawns, interspersed with rustic wooden benches at regular intervals. A horseshoe of pastel cottage-style houses framed the communal area.

As she made her way to the address PI Fischer had sent her, Haley nodded and smiled at the elderly residents strolling past her along the walkways, some with small, elab-orately-coiffed dogs on leashes. Taking a deep breath, she raised her hand to rap her knuckles on the front door of cottage 207, but before she could do so, a birdlike voice from behind startled her. "Can I help you, dear?"

Haley spun around and stared at the diminutive silver-haired woman leaning on a stick who had walked up behind her. Gentle creases in the woman's face curved into a ques-tioning smile.

Haley's mouth opened and then closed again as she strug-gled for the right words to introduce herself to the woman she assumed must be her mother-in-law. "Hi, I'm Haley Wilder," she blurted out.

One of the woman's thin eyebrows inched upward. "Do I have an appointment with you?"

Before Haley could answer, a plump woman ambled by huffing and puffing. "Morning, Caroline," she called out cheerily.

Jake's mother turned and waved back at her. "Morning, Jan. See you at the bridge game tonight." She fixed her attention back on Haley. "I'm sorry to keep you waiting, dear. Are you the new resident assistant?"

"Uh, no, I'm not, but I do have something important to discuss with you if you can spare a moment."

Caroline rubbed her brow distractedly. "Yes, of course. What did you say your name was again?"

"Haley, Haley Wilder."

"Ah, yes, that's right. Forgive me, I'm a tad forgetful at times." As she poked a bony finger at the numeric keypad to open up her front door, Haley tried to calm her racing heart and reorient her thoughts. Caroline hadn't recognized her married name, which indicated she had no idea her son had changed his name. Haley would have to tread carefully. If Caroline was estranged from her son, it wasn't likely she would want anything to do with a daughter-in-law either.

Haley followed her inside the cottage and sat down in the plush wing-back chair Caroline pointed her to. "I'll just let my husband, Ronnie, know I'm back," she said. "He wasn't feeling too good this morning, so he stayed in bed instead of accompanying me on my walk."

As soon as Caroline exited the room, Haley's eyes drifted around the space, her gaze settling on a photo frame on the window sill. She got to her feet and walked over to it. After a moment's hesitation, she picked it up and examined it more closely. Her breath caught in her throat. It was Jake and his brother as young teens, each with a fishing pole in hand, grinning broadly at the camera as they held up their prized catch. She couldn't tell from looking at the photograph which of them was older, but Travis was a couple of inches taller than Jake—or *Dillon* as he'd been called back then. She startled when Caroline reappeared in the doorway and hastily replaced the photo frame on the window sill.

"That's a great photo," Haley offered.

Caroline beamed at her. "Yes, those are my sons, Travis and Dillon." She rubbed a crooked finger over her brow and peered at Haley. "I'm sorry, did you say you were the new resident assistant?"

"No, I'm not." Haley fixed a patient smile on her face. "Why don't you take a seat and I'll explain why I'm here."

"I haven't even offered you a cup of coffee, or would you prefer tea?" Caroline asked as she made her way over to the love seat. "I was going to make one for Ronnie but he's still sleeping."

"Maybe later, thanks," Haley answered. "For now, I'd really like to talk to you about something."

Caroline deposited her petite frame in the love seat and then leaned back, adjusting a cushion behind her. "This sounds serious," she said, with a twinkle in her eye. "I hope Ronnie hasn't been causing trouble on the golf course again. I keep telling him not to talk politics. It just gets everyone all riled up and next thing you know they're throwing their clubs at one another and not speaking anymore."

Haley shook her head. "Caroline, I'm not on staff here. I'm your daughter-in-law. I'm married to your son Dillon. Except he doesn't go by that name anymore. I've only ever known him as Jake Wilder."

Caroline blinked in confusion, rubbing her knotted hands together. "But Dillon ... isn't married." She drew her thin brows together in concentration. "Travis married a nice girl, but they divorced two years later. Such a shame. I was looking forward to having grandchildren, but it wasn't meant to be, I suppose."

"Dillon and I got married nine months ago." Haley pulled out a wedding photograph and handed it to her. "We live two hours from here."

Caroline's lips parted and she blinked uncomprehendingly. "But ... I don't understand. Why didn't Dillon tell us he was getting married?"

Haley hesitated, reluctant to distress the elderly woman any further by adding that Dillon had lied and said his mother was dead. "I'm afraid I don't have a good answer for you. When was the last time you saw him?"

"Well, it's been a while." Caroline wrinkled her brow in concentration. "He visited us at Christmas. Both boys stopped by."

Haley's pulse pounded an ominous beat in her temples at the news. By all appearances, the brothers weren't estranged after all. "Do you have any idea why Dillon might have changed his name?"

Caroline's face fell. A lone tear rolled down the creases in her cheeks. "I really don't know what's going on with those boys. They hardly ever come to see us anymore. It's been so hard for them, you see, they just can't let it go. Ronnie and I have accepted it and moved on as best we can under the circumstances." She let out a long, shuddering sigh. "But the boys have never been the same since their sister hung herself."

*B*listering fear rippled down Haley's spine. *Sister?* Her mind worked furiously to piece it all together. It couldn't be Emma, could it? *You think you got away with it, don't you?* Had Jake sent all those messages? Her jaw wobbled as she tried to speak. "Jake—I mean, Dillon, never mentioned anything about ... a sister." Even as the words fell from her lips, she realized the absurdity of them. Of course, he hadn't. He'd never talked about a brother either, and the little he'd told her about his parents was a lie. In fact, he'd lied about everything. Haley felt hollow inside. Was their entire life together a sham? Was his professed love for her a farce played out to lure her into his trap?

Caroline stared back at her, a perturbed frown on her forehead. She raised a gnarled hand to her temple and carefully smoothed a thin strand of gray hair back from her face. "Well, I imagine it would have been hard for Dillon to talk to you about his sister. He never talks about her to anyone. Travis and Dillon were both devastated when she died. They were a good bit older, you see, my first husband's kids. Max passed away when they were only little. They kept his last name—Ramsey. I married Ronnie the following year, and our daughter was born a few years after that. The boys adored her—they were very protective of their little sister."

Caroline got to her feet and shuffled over to a display cabinet next to the television. She opened a glass door and lifted down a small silver photo frame. After studying it for a moment, she hobbled back across the room and handed it to Haley with a sad smile. "That's our Em on her first day of kindergarten."

Haley's hand shook so hard she could barely grasp the photo frame. "Em? Is that ... is that short for Emma?"

Caroline chuckled. "Emmeline, but she always hated it—said it was old-fashioned. She went by Em, or Emma."

Haley's mind flashed back to her sophomore year and the first time the quad sisters had set eyes on Emma Murray. They'd sized her up pretty quickly, marked her as easy prey. Attractive, not stunning, shy enough for them to inflict some serious damage. She had never stood a chance. Haley grimaced. They hadn't thought of her as someone's daughter, or sister, only as the object of their amusement. Haley mustered her courage to ask the question burning on her lips. "How old was your daughter when she hanged herself?"

"She was only fifteen." Caroline shook her head, dropping her gaze to the floor momentarily. "It broke our hearts. She had so much potential, so much to live for. Emma could play the piano beautifully and she used to write all her own music. Poetry too. She was a very sensitive child—the kindest person I've ever known. She wanted to be an environmentalist. She had a big heart for animals."

Haley winced, each reminder of the life snuffed out like another slash across her chest. Her head swam with memories coming thick and fast. Emma's diary pouring out her hopes and dreams, her tender spirit that had shown so much care and concern for the world around her. Haley handed back the photo frame with trembling fingers, unable to bring herself to ask what high school Emma had attended. She couldn't risk Caroline posing the same question to her. But she needed to be absolutely certain this wasn't all a horrible coincidence—some desperate part of her still hoping against hope that it wasn't the same Emma. After all, thousands of teenagers attempted suicide every year. Haley sucked in a silent breath. "Do you have a picture of Emma when she was older?"

Wordlessly, Caroline returned to the cabinet and retrieved another frame. She handed it to Haley with a heavy sigh. "This is the last photo I have of her. Ronnie took it on her fifteenth birthday."

Haley scrutinized the shoulder-length brown hair, the big blue eyes framed by thick lashes, lips so similar in shape to the ones she'd kissed a thousand times it almost took her breath away. How had she not seen a resemblance between Jake and Emma before? Maybe it was because she'd tried so hard to blot out the memory of the girl whose life she'd destroyed. Now, that memory was back with a vengeance. Her throat began to close over, her voice an uncomfortable rasp, as the horror of what was unfolding began to sink in. Her husband was Emma Murray's brother. He and his brother had hunted down their sister's killer, fully intent on revenge. The room began to spin around her. She had to get out of here. It wasn't safe to stay here any longer. "Could I get a glass of water, please?"

"Yes, of course, dear," Caroline replied, getting to her feet. "I'm sorry if I upset you. I shouldn't have brought it up."

She disappeared into the kitchen, and Haley reached for a magazine from a rack next to the couch and examined the mailing label.

Caroline Murray, 207 Sunrise Manor.

There it was in black and white. Caroline was Emma

Murray's mother. Haley stared at the photo of fifteen-year-old Emma trying to decide what to do. The truth was staring her in the face. Jake, the man she'd promised to love, honor, and cherish until death, had set out to punish her for the unforgivable sin she had committed. And now she was in his clutches. There was no telling how far he planned to take his campaign of terror against her, but all indications were that he wasn't going to rest until she was dead.

Confusion and terror swirled around inside her brain. Sooner or later, Jake would find out she'd visited his parents and discovered the truth about him. She wasn't safe in her own home—she hadn't been safe since the day she met him. Hurriedly scrolling through her contacts, she pulled up Detective Tillet's number. She needed to bring him up to speed on everything as quickly as possible.

Caroline reappeared in the doorway holding a glass of water. Haley got to her feet, downed it and handed it back gratefully. "I'm so sorry, Caroline, but I really need to head home. Dillon's expecting me back for dinner. Please don't mention to him that I stopped by. I'm sure he'd rather explain to you himself why he hasn't told you yet that we're married. He might be upset if he knew I'd been here."

Caroline puckered her brow. "I can't for the life of me think why he kept something like this from Ronnie and me. We would have been happy for him—for you both, dear. We always wanted him and Travis to move on with their lives. Travis, in particular, couldn't come to terms with what happened. He even threatened to kill himself on multiple occasions. You can imagine how worried we've been about the boys all these years."

Haley wrestled with how to respond. She couldn't possibly tell Caroline the truth—that her marriage was a sham, and Dillon a monster. She laid a hand on her mother-in-law's arm. "He was probably just trying to protect you.

Maybe he didn't want you to think I was a replacement for Emma. I'm sure Dillon would have told you all about me in good time."

Caroline nodded absently. "Yes, I suppose you're right, dear. I hope to see you again soon—Ronnie will want to meet you too. Drive safely. I really don't like the idea of you navigating the freeway at rush hour all by yourself."

Haley gave her a wan smile. "Don't worry, I'll be careful. And thanks for your hospitality." She couldn't bring herself to say that she was looking forward to seeing her mother-in-law again too. If she got out of this situation alive, they would never meet again.

Back in the safety of her car, Haley immediately dialed Detective Tillet's number. The phone rang several times, and panic streaked through her as she started up her car and pulled out of the parking lot. What if he was off duty? What if she couldn't reach him until it was too late? Seconds dragged by before he answered.

"Detective Tillet speaking."

"It's Haley Wilder," she blurted out. "I know who the stalker is—stalkers."

The words tumbled from her lips as she filled him in on everything she'd found out.

"You have to think through your next steps carefully," Detective Tillet said when she was finished. "It's going to take some time to gather enough evidence to make a case against your husband and his brother. In the meantime, it isn't safe for you to return home. Do you have somewhere else you can go? Someplace they won't be able to find you?"

"I could stay with my friend, Natalie," Haley suggested. "Jake doesn't know where she lives."

"You'll need to come up with a believable excuse for not going home. You can't do anything to alert your husband that you're on to him."

Haley chewed on her nail. "I'll tell him my mother has taken ill and I'm flying to Florida to visit her in the hospital."

"That should work," Detective Tillet said. "Keep a low profile and take a few days off work. And don't leave your friend's house if you can help it."

"I'm just getting on the freeway now. I need to swing by my place first and pick up my dog, Katniss. I'll tell Jake I'm dropping her at the boarding kennel on my way to the airport. I don't trust him to take care of her."

"It would be better if you didn't go home at all. Can't you get your friend to go by your house for you?"

"No, if Jake checks the security cameras and sees Natalie, he'll know I was lying to him. Don't worry, I'll call his office and make sure he's there before I pick up Katniss."

"All right," Detective Tillet agreed with some reluctance. "Let me know as soon as you're safely at your friend's house."

Haley ended the call and immediately dialed Jake's office. "Hey, Rochelle, it's Haley. I wanted to stop by and drop something off for Jake. Is he working in the office today?"

"Yes, he's here."

"Great, don't mention it to him. It's a surprise."

"No problem," Rochelle said with a conspiratorial chuckle. "My lips are sealed."

Haley set the cruise control and called Natalie's number next, resigned to finally telling her the truth—something she should have done a long time ago.

"Hey, Hales," Natalie chirped. "I was wondering where you were. It's not like you to take two personal days in a row. Is everything okay?"

"No," Haley replied. "Far from it. It's time I told you the truth about what's been going on." With a tremulous waver in her voice she began to recount the whole ugly story on the long drive home.

For once, Natalie remained subdued and let Haley do the

talking. When she was finished, Natalie promptly offered to do whatever she could to help. "Of course you can stay at my place as long as you want. What they're doing to you is horrific—it's criminal."

Tears stung Haley's eyes at her compassion. Natalie was the kind of friend she wished she'd been years ago when Emma needed her most.

By the time Haley exited the freeway, she and Natalie had firmed up a plan. Natalie explained where the spare key to her apartment was and how to sneak Katniss into the building to avoid the security cameras. Her apartment complex didn't allow pets, but under the circumstances, Haley had convinced her it would be safer if Katniss stayed with them until Detective Tillet could make an arrest.

As Haley pulled into her cul-de-sac, she saw the customary curtain twitch in her neighbor's house. She twisted her lips in a grimace. How ironic that she'd shared her suspicions about Harold with Jake. It was almost impossible to process the idea that her husband, the one person she thought would always protect her, was actually the monster who'd been tormenting her all along. For now, she had to do her best to compartmentalize that fact and concentrate on staying alive until Detective Tillet could piece together the evidence he needed to obtain arrest warrants for both brothers.

Haley parked in her driveway, walked up to the front door and disarmed the alarm. She needed to work quickly. Once she was safely out of the house, she would make the call to Jake to let him know her mother had fallen gravely ill and that she was catching a flight to Florida.

She set down her purse on the hall table, and made her way to the kitchen to greet Katniss. The room was eerily quiet and her German shepherd was nowhere to be seen. Haley's stomach gave a sickening lurch. Surely Jake wouldn't harm the dog, would he? She peered anxiously out into the backyard, and whistled for her. To her relief, Katniss lifted her head from sniffing at something beneath a bush at the far end of the garden. She bounded excitedly toward her, surprised to see her home in the middle of the day.

"Good girl, Kat!" Haley gushed, ruffling her ears. She wasted no time gathering together a few essentials, including a leash and a bag of dog food. "Wait here," she said, patting the dog's head. "I need to grab a few things for myself."

As she turned to head for the stairs, Katniss emitted a low growl at the back of her throat. Haley came to a sudden halt and looked down at her questioningly. "What is it, Kat? What's wrong?"

Katniss bared her fangs and growled again, more menacingly this time. Sensing movement behind her, Haley spun around, and froze.

"Hello, Haley. We haven't officially met yet. I figured it was time to introduce myself."

A tall, bearded man with Jake's piercing eyes blocked Haley's exit. A sneer crept across his hate-filled face. "Aren't you going to say hello to your brother-in-law?"

Haley took a shaky step backward, her knees almost buckling beneath her. *It was him! Travis!*

Everything that happened next was a blur of color and confusion. Katniss let out a savage snarl and leapt toward him. But he'd come prepared. Quick as a flash, he deployed a stun baton. Katniss howled in pain as she flew backward, retreating to the kitchen where she rolled around on the floor yelping the most unimaginable sounds that ripped at Haley's heartstrings. Travis slammed the kitchen door shut on the injured dog and grabbed Haley by the hair, holding the stun baton threateningly close to her cheek. "You're gonna do exactly what I tell you to do, or you'll be next in line for a little shock treatment."

Haley moaned softly in response, nodding her head slightly to show that she understood. There was no point in attempting her fledgling self-defense moves with a stun baton hovering inches from her face. Travis wasn't in the mood to be challenged. She'd only end up incapacitated and writhing around in agony like Katniss. Her mind swirled with a slew of unanswered questions. How did he know she would be at the house? Had Caroline called him? Was she in on it too? All that talk of her boys rarely coming around anymore might have been a pack of lies. As sweet as she'd come across, she might be equally as vengeful and devious as her sons. Maybe she believed what Haley had done to her daughter justified this course of action.

"Why are you doing this?" Haley gasped.

Travis let out a contemptuous snort. "You already know the answer to that. You've been doing enough digging around at Sunrise Manor today to put two and two together."

Haley sucked in an icy breath. "How did you know I visited your mother? Did she tell you?"

Travis gave a scathing laugh. "I knew you were there before she did. I installed a security camera at her house that's linked to an app on my phone. I needed to stay on top of things in case you ever figured it out. Our mother has no idea you're the one who killed Emma. And even if we told her, she wouldn't approve of us teaching you a lesson you'll never forget."

"We?" Haley echoed, fear radiating through her.

"Dillon and I made a pact years ago to avenge Emma's death," Travis said, his expression darkening. "It took us a long time to eliminate everyone in the school. Believe me, we had to date a lot of girls to get the information we needed. But as it turns out, there's always someone who can't keep their mouth shut. Now that we finally know who's responsible for driving Emma to kill herself, it's time for retribution. We'll tackle the quad squad one at a time, but first we're going to deal with the ringleader. After all, you're the one who put the nail in her coffin the day you pinned her diary page to the noticeboard."

Terror ricocheted around inside Haley's head. Jake had been in on everything from the start. He'd sat at the bar that first night watching her, raising his tumbler in her direction, waiting to make his move. Her husband, the man she loved, had married her so he could destroy her slowly from the inside out.

"It's a real shame you cut our time together short by sticking your nose in where it didn't belong—I wanted to watch you self-destruct a little more first," Travis drawled.

"Please don't do this," Haley cajoled, her heart thundering beneath her ribs. "We were just a bunch of stupid teenagers. It was only supposed to be a silly prank. We never imagined Emma would react the way she did. I didn't intend her any harm."

"Your intentions don't interest me," Travis replied, his eyes hard and cold as they bored into her like daggers. "My sister died because of your merciless campaign of terror against her. And now it's time for you to learn a few lessons in fear, the kind of fear that drives a girl to kill herself. It would be a fitting end if you hanged yourself too, but that's too good a death for you. We're going to do things a little differently."

Haley's stomach knotted at the ominous threat. She stumbled backward in a bid to get away, but Travis held her roughly upright. "Listen to me very carefully. You're going to walk out to your car, get in the driver's seat and put both hands on the wheel. If you attempt to run or scream or do anything else that draws any attention to us, I'll bundle you into the car and take you to an undisclosed location and make sure no one ever hears of you again. After that, I'll come back here and finish off your dog."

"No! Please don't," Haley whispered. "Leave Katniss out of this."

By way of response, Travis shoved her toward the front

door. She eyed her purse on the hall table despairingly. Her phone was a tantalizing couple of feet away. Detective Tillet would know something was wrong when she didn't call him, but by then it might be too late. He had no idea she was with Travis, and he had no way of tracking her.

"You won't get away with this," Haley said trying to hold her voice steady. "Detective Tillet is on his way. And your face is on my security camera hard drive now."

"Your camera's disarmed, *sweetheart*. Isn't that what our Dillon calls you?" Travis threw back his head and laughed raucously. "My face isn't on the hard drive, and neither is yours. In fact, there's nothing to indicate you came back here today." He shoved her forward, bundling a scarf around his neck and over his mouth. "Now, open the door and walk to your car, keep your eyes down. Don't attempt to make contact with anyone."

Fingers shaking, Haley opened her front door. She was sorely tempted to glance to the left, hoping to catch Edith Moore looking out from behind her curtain. Maybe she could give her a signal of some kind. Her heart sank at the hopelessness of that thought. The old woman was half blind. She wouldn't know what was going on. She'd think it was Jake accompanying her to the car. Haley realized with a start that it must have been Travis who Edith saw the day the fruit basket was delivered to her doorstep. He looked so similar to his brother, it would be impossible to tell them apart from Edith's vantage point, especially if he'd been wearing a scarf that day too. Fighting back a wave of nausea, Haley opened her car door and climbed in. Travis slid into the passenger seat next to her and thumped the stun baton against the palm of his hand. "Now, drive."

As they exited the sub-division, Haley scanned the occupants of approaching cars, trying to spot someone she knew, hoping she could send a message with her distraught eyes that would alert them to the fact that something was desperately wrong. With a sinking feeling in her heart, she realized that even if she did pass someone she recognized, they'd assume at a cursory glance that it was Jake sitting next to her. No one was going to intervene in her abduction. She was completely on her own.

Within minutes, they'd left the subdivision behind and were on the freeway heading south. Haley held the steering wheel in a death grip as she tried in vain to think of a plan to get away from Travis. She glanced at the fuel gauge, but thanks to her methodical habit of filling it up once the needle went below the halfway mark, it was close to full. Maybe she could tell him she needed to use the restroom and make a run for it while they were stopped. She would have to fashion a meticulous plan to pull that off. Her mind raced through one frightening scenario after another. She wondered if Jake was still working in his office. Did he even know his brother had kidnapped her? She still wasn't entirely sure she believed everything Travis had told her. It was far too painful to think that Jake wanted her dead.

Spotting a sign for services at the next exit, she made a show of squirming in her seat. "I need to use the bathroom."

Travis kept his eyes forward. "Tough luck."

"I can't hold it for much longer," Haley whined.

"We're not stopping so deal with it."

"I'm telling you, I can't!" Haley yelled.

"All right!" Travis thumped his fist on the dashboard. "There's a rest stop a half hour or so farther south. We'll pull over there."

"But—"

"Just shut up and keep driving!"

Haley flinched at the raw anger in his voice. She was only too aware that he was still holding the stun baton in his lap. It was anyone's guess what else he might be concealing inside his jacket. It wasn't worth risking stoking his anger. She wondered if Detective Tillet was growing concerned yet about her whereabouts. No doubt he'd tried to call her by now. Natalie might have been trying to get in touch with her too. Haley thought of her parents and tears pricked her eyes. Now, she regretted not calling them more often and keeping them apprised of what was happening. Would she ever see them or hear their voices again?

Travis's phone began to ring. He shot Haley a warning glance before fishing it out of his pocket. "Yeah, yeah I got her. No, not yet."

Haley's stomach twisted. Was he talking to her husband, *Dillon?*

"See you there. Yeah, bye." Travis ended the call and slipped his phone back into his pocket. He pointed to a sign indicating a rest stop one mile ahead. "You can pull off now."

Wordlessly, Haley turned the wheel and exited the freeway, she wasn't about to waste an opportunity to try and escape. Surely there must be a trucker or two around, if nothing else. A flicker of hope shot through her when she pulled into the rest stop and spotted two semi-trucks lined up on one side of the parking lot. The curtains were drawn on the cabs, but it was comforting to know that there were other people in the vicinity at least. She'd have to think through any escape attempt carefully. If she started screaming for help, the truckers might not wake up in time to stop Travis from stunning her and dragging her back to the car. She needed a better plan. She switched off the engine and turned to him. "Can I get out now?"

He narrowed his eyes at her, inching the stun baton closer. "Just remember, if you yell for help, or make any stupid moves, you're riding in the trunk the rest of the way."

Opening the passenger door, he climbed out and shadowed her as she made her way to the women's bathroom. To her horror, he followed her inside.

"What are you doing?" she demanded. "How about a little privacy?"

"I'm making sure you don't try anything stupid, like up and disappear on me," he said, sticking his face up to hers. "Now get a move on. We don't have all day." Leaning up against a filthy sink, he folded his arms in front of him and stared defiantly at her.

Haley took a quick calming breath and darted a glance around the dingy, stained restroom. There was no exit, only a small vent too high up on the wall to be of any use. She went into the stall farthest from Travis, locked it, and leaned against the door, trying to think. Her only chance was to make a run for it once she exited the restroom. She could leg it across to the closest semi-truck and bang on the door—if she made it that far. Even if Travis used his stun baton on her, he might not have time to drag her all the way back to her car before one of the truckers came out to see what all the ruckus was about. And, with a bit of luck, the trucker might be more than a match for Travis. She had to believe most truckers carried a handgun in their cab for protection. At the very least, they could call the police on her behalf and tell the other truckers on the road to keep an eye out for her vehicle. It was a desperate plan, but it was her only shot.

Her mind made up, she flushed the toilet and opened the door, tossing an insolent glance at Travis as she washed her hands. When the dryer switched off, she stalked past him, but before she could exit the restroom her right arm was wrenched backward.

"Not so fast," he snarled. He wrapped his arms tightly around her waist holding the stun baton inches from her body. "We'll walk out together, just in case you're planning any funny business."

Haley swallowed back the bile rising up her throat as she eyed the baton. It wouldn't do any good to try and break away from Travis's pincer-like hold. He'd immobilize her in seconds. Reluctantly, she allowed herself to be marched back to her car, where Travis shoved her unceremoniously into the driver's seat.

"Get back on the freeway," he growled. "Keep heading south. We've got another hour to go."

Haley gritted her teeth in frustration, but there was nothing else to do but to keep driving to wherever he was taking her. They didn't exchange another word until Travis ordered her to take the next exit. They drove through a small town, a smattering of businesses on either side of the road, and then turned onto a gravel road. They were well out in the countryside now, in a rural area unfamiliar to Haley. She drove along the potholed road for another couple of miles until Travis instructed her to pull off to the side.

Haley looked around anxiously. "Why are we stopping here?"

"I'm driving the rest of the way,." Travis reached into the glove box and pulled out a long, black scarf. "Tie this over your eyes."

Haley recoiled. "No! I don't want to—"

Her voice cut off abruptly as pain ricocheted through her body. Her muscles seized up and she slumped to one side, momentarily rendered immobile by the stun baton in Travis's hand. She lay across the seat moaning, powerless to resist him as he fastened the blindfold around her eyes and then duct taped it to her face, blacking out daylight. He pulled her wrists in front of her and secured them with a zip tie before pulling her roughly to her feet and half-dragging her around to the back of the car.

Before she fully grasped what was happening, he'd tossed her into the trunk and slammed the lid closed.

For the next excruciating mile or so, the car bumped up and down mercilessly over the rutted road. Haley did what little she could to protect herself from the violent jolting by bracing her legs against the sides of the trunk. She had no idea where they were headed, but Travis had done a good job of making sure she wouldn't be able to lead anyone back here, even if she did somehow manage to escape.

At last, the car rolled to a stop and the engine cut out. A cold sweat clung to the back of Haley's neck. She waited uneasily for what would happen next, her muscles cramping up. Travis left her trapped for another ten or fifteen minutes before finally opening the truck and hauling her to her feet. The ground beneath her was uneven, and she almost stumbled when he shoved her roughly forward. When she came to a stop, he unceremoniously wrenched the blindfold down around her neck, ripping strands of her hair out along with the duct tape stuck to her forehead.

Her heart sank as she took in her surroundings. Woodlands stretched out in every direction as far as the eye could see. In front of her stood a filthy, dilapidated trailer surrounded by the remnants of a chain link fence, a collection of old tires, a rusted deck chair, and a couple of broken plant pots.

Travis watched her reaction with relish. "Welcome to your new abode. Don't worry, it's only temporary." He laughed as if at some private joke, and then opened the torn screen door and elbowed her up the steps.

Inside, the grungy space was moldy and smelled like something was decaying. Stuffing peeked through the couch cushions, and the tiny windows were coated with a thick layer of grime the color of pond scum. Haley suspected that animals might have been living inside the trailer, although the dark, shag carpet was so filthy, it was impossible to say for sure. The back of the trailer sported a queen-sized bed with a frayed duvet, a pile of rank-smelling clothing, and miscellaneous items. A fresh wave of panic washed over her. She didn't relish the idea of being forced to sleep on the unsanitary bed, but it was unlikely Travis would let her sleep on the couch next to the door, *if* he let her live through the night.

Without warning, he shoved her down on the sagging couch. She yelped as her shoulder banged up against the side of a cabinet. "Why are you doing this to me?"

"Like I told you, it's time to pay for your crime. You thought you got away with killing Emma years ago, but she had people who loved her, brothers who vowed to protect her. Only we couldn't because of what you did. You took her from us. All that's left for us is to avenge her."

Haley stared at him, her throat bobbing with trepidation as she formed the question that was burning inside her. "Is … Dillon really in on this with you?"

Travis threw her a scathing look. "You killed his baby sister. What do you think?"

Shame and terror blended as one in Haley's heart. "I feel sick about what happened, but I didn't kill your sister. She did that to herself. I admit I'm the one who posted a page of her diary on a notice board. It was a dumb thing to do and I deeply regret the pain it caused her. I've had to live with what I did all these years. Believe me, if I could take it back, I would."

"But you can't, and that's the problem," Travis cut in. "Now it's time for retribution. An eye for an eye."

"Please, I'm begging you to let me go, Travis. I didn't know what I was doing. I wasn't the same person back then. I was insecure and desperate for friends—I only did it to try and impress people, like teenagers do."

"I couldn't care less about your lousy sob story," Travis hissed. "If that's your only excuse for the way you treated Emma, then you don't deserve to live."

Haley opened her mouth to respond, but the sound of a vehicle pulling up outside the trailer silenced her. She stiffened. Was it Jake—Dillon—as she'd have to refer to him now? It almost seemed easier not to call him Jake. It was too much of a disconnect to think that the man she'd lived with for the past nine months was committed to destroying her, killing her even. A tremor of fear rippled across her shoulders. Would they take it that far? Travis had hinted as much. But surely her husband wouldn't allow it.

Or would he?

A car door slammed, and then footsteps trudged toward the trailer and up the steps. The screen door creaked outward and a shadow filled the doorway. Haley sucked in a sharp breath. Dillon's steely eyes locked onto hers signaling a hatred she could scarcely fathom.

"Ja— Dillon! Please help me!" she cried. "You don't have to do this!"

Ignoring her, he addressed his brother. "No run-ins with that detective I warned you about?"

"No, just the dog. I had to stun it."

Dillon curled his lip. "You should have finished it off while you were at it."

"We'll worry about the mutt afterward," Travis replied. "Did you get the supplies?"

"No time. My nosy neighbor was peeking around her curtain, watching my every move."

Travis narrowed his eyes at Dillon. "You were supposed to get everything out of the garage and bring it with you."

Dillon shrugged. "I'll run into town and grab some shovels and a tarp."

"We agreed not to show our faces in town," Travis snapped.

"It won't be a problem. I'll wear a beanie and shades."

Haley sucked in a sharp breath, her heart quaking in her chest. There was no mistaking the intent. They were planning on killing her and burying her out here in the woods.

Travis scowled. "Don't be long. We need to finish this tonight."

Dillon threw Haley a darting look as he strode to the door. "Just make sure she doesn't go anywhere until I get back." He let the screen door slam behind him and, moments later, Haley heard the sound of an engine starting up. An unfamiliar dark green sedan pulled away from the trailer. Haley grimaced. A rental, no doubt. Dillon had thought of every detail—just in case there was a trace out on his car.

A hollow silence filled the trailer. She glanced across at Travis with trepidation, waiting for him to speak, terrified of what he'd say next.

His gaze bored into her. "You thought you got away with it, didn't you? You're sick in the head, you know that? Now you're finally going to learn that the way you treat people always comes back to haunt you in the end. And this is the end of the road for you."

Haley shrank back from him in terror. "I'm begging you not to go through with this. I can't believe Jake would go along—"

"His ... name's ... not ... Jake," Travis screamed in her face. "It's Dillon Ramsey, Emma's brother."

"Okay, you're right, but he's still my husband—"

Travis cut her off with a caustic laugh. "He was never your husband."

Tears streamed down Haley's cheeks. "Then why did he marry me?"

"It wasn't the original plan. But when you fell for him, we realized how advantageous it would be to have complete access to your life. A marriage of convenience so we could dismantle you from within, strip away your hopes, and dreams, your future—just like you did to Emma."

Haley suppressed a sob. "I never wanted her to kill herself. You have to believe me."

"I don't have to believe anything *you* tell me. But I do believe what everyone else at your school had to say about you—spoiled, conceited, contemptuous, devious, dangerous. You were a callous cow back then, and that's all you'll ever be."

"That's not true, Travis! People change. That's not who I am anymore—that's not who I ever really was. I was trying too hard to fit in. I'm ashamed of what I did, I've spent my life trying to make amends ever since."

"Too late for Emma, isn't it? You took her life, and you destroyed my parents' lives, and my life, and my brother's. Sorry isn't going to cut it. Justice demands a life for a life."

Haley shrank back from the spittle hovering on Travis's lips. He was strikingly like her husband, and yet unrecognizable in other ways, a darkness brooding in his eyes that struck terror in her heart. It was beginning to sink in that she wasn't going to leave this trailer alive, not if the brothers had their way. They had hunted her down like crazed killers—put their own lives on hold so they could infiltrate hers long enough to destroy it. Dillon had even allowed Travis to beat him up to throw her off the trail. They'd taken everything from her, including her dream of a happy marriage. And judging by the supplies Dillon had gone into town to pick up, she may not have long before they took her life too.

Somehow, she had to find a way to break out of the trailer. Detective Tillet would never find her in time to save her. Her best bet was to try and escape before her husband returned from town. Despite her self-defense training, she couldn't possibly take on both brothers at once. Squeezing her eyes shut, she tried to clear her brain of the panic rapidly turning it to mush. The bathroom was the only place in the trailer that offered any privacy, and the possibility of escape. If she could free her hands, she might be able to climb out through the vent on the roof. It was a long shot, but maybe this time she could pull it off. She squirmed on the couch for a minute or two, then said abruptly, "I need to use the bathroom."

"Just shut up and wait till Dillon gets back."

Haley grimaced. "I can't hold it. My stomach's upset. This trailer's going to stink even worse than it already does if you make me sit here any longer."

Travis glanced up from his phone, his brow creasing with distaste. "Whatever," he growled, gesturing with a tilt of his chin to the tiny door halfway between the couch and the bed. "Make it quick."

Slowly, Haley got to her feet and walked over to the bathroom door. She placed her bound hands on the handle and twisted it open, holding her breath when she caught sight of the plastic vent on the roof. It was just about big enough for her to squeeze through if she could make it up there. She closed the bathroom door behind her and quietly locked it. After turning on the faucet, she opened the cabinet above the sink and began looking for a pair of scissors or something else she could use to cut the zip tie around her wrists. Her frantic search of the cabinet turned up nothing other than a handful of out-of-date toiletries and a foul-smelling toothbrush. Growing more frantic with every passing second, she knelt and opened the tiny cupboard beneath the sink. A few rolls of toilet paper and some cleaning supplies were wedged around the plastic pipes. In desperation, she grabbed the tiny trashcan and rummaged through it. Her heart jolted at the sight of a rusted razor blade glinting among the trash. Gingerly, she fished it out and began to saw at the zip tie. Sweat trickled down the back of her neck.

"What are you doing in there? Hurry up!" Travis yelled.

Haley bit her lip, tasting blood. From the sound of his voice she could tell he hadn't ventured any closer to the bathroom.

"I told you my stomach's upset," she hollered back. "I need a few more minutes."

She swiped at a strand of hair that had fallen across her face and frantically went back to work sawing at the zip tie. After a couple more seconds, it finally popped apart. She tossed it in the garbage can along with the razor blade, and then slipped off her heels, climbed up on the toilet lid and reached for the vent above. Opening it all the way, she gritted her teeth as she prepared to pull herself up, bracing her legs against two walls of the tiny bathroom. It took all of her willpower not to grunt out loud as she inched her way painfully upward. With a final burst of energy, she pulled herself through the vent, trying desperately not to rattle it. Free at last, she stuck her head back down into the tiny bathroom and called out, "Almost done." Gingerly, she began crawling on her hands and knees along the trailer roof through the half-mulched leaves and debris that had accumulated up top.

When she got to the far end of the trailer, she set about making her way down the rungs of the tiny iron ladder next to the spare tire. Her foot caught in something and she reached for it to free herself. Her eyes widened in disbelief. A rope noose hung from the ladder. Her heart thudded halfway up her throat. Was it meant for her? She hurriedly continued down the ladder, trying not to retch at the thought of her lifeless body hanging from the noose. Travis had said hanging would be too good a death for her. Maybe they were planning to taunt her with the rope before they killed her by some other equally gruesome method.

Stepping onto solid ground at last, she exhaled softly and glanced around, searching for something she could use as a weapon. There was no way she could outrun Travis in her bare feet, and she was reluctant to make a dash for her car when she wasn't sure if he'd left the keys in it. She had to immobilize him first. Her best shot was to hide alongside the trailer and surprise him when he came out to look for her, which would happen any minute now once he realized she wasn't in the bathroom anymore.

Her eyes scanned the junk surrounding the trailer. She might have only seconds to find something she could wield as a weapon. Her gaze fell on a piece of concrete behind one of the trailer tires. It was more unwieldy than she'd have liked, but it would serve her purpose. All that was left was to wait in the shadows and strike before he found her.

29

*H*unkering down, Haley reached for the concrete block and began to creep cautiously around to the front of the trailer, staying low and out of sight of the door. Her skin crawled as she thought about what she had to do next. But there was no other way out of this situation. Travis and Dillon had made it clear they would show no mercy now that they had her in their clutches.

Suddenly she heard yelling and then the sound of Travis's fists hammering on the bathroom door. Muscles tensed, she sucked in her breath and waited for him to appear in the doorway. Seconds later, the screen door flew open and Travis tore down the steps in a single leap, brandishing the stun baton. Haley swallowed the hard knot in her throat. She dreaded the thought of hurting another human being, but she had to stay committed to doing what she needed to do to save herself. She couldn't allow herself to think of Travis as anything other than a stalker who fully intended to kill her and bury her body in the middle of nowhere.

Her thoughts flashed to her parents and what it would do to them if their only child vanished without a trace, never to be heard of again. Her circle of friends was small, but Natalie would be devastated, and even her hard-nosed boss, Nick—who had taught her so much in such a short span of time—would miss her. Katniss of course would be broken-hearted. Tears pricked at Haley's eyes. She didn't want to die. She didn't want to kill Travis either, but if it came down to it, she wouldn't succumb without a fight.

When he came racing around the side of the trailer, Haley sprang at him in a catlike movement, smashing the brick into his skull. He dropped without as much as a grunt, stunned by the ferocity of the blow she'd unleashed, but surprisingly not rendered unconscious. He blinked up at her as he lay on the ground at her feet, trying to orient himself before struggling to his knees. Haley didn't wait to watch his progress. She turned and darted to her car.

Wrenching open the driver's door, hope soared inside her when she saw the keys in the ignition. But before she could slide into the seat, she felt the heavy weight of Travis's hand clawing at her shoulder. Every instinct in her body rebelled against allowing him to overpower her. Haruki's smooth voice came to mind, silently coaching her through her moves. Drawing on her training, she spun and kicked Travis in the groin with as much speed and strength as she could muster. He fell to his knees again, emitting a guttural groan. Without a second's delay, Haley scrambled into her car and turned the key, fingers trembling so hard she could scarcely grip the wheel. Slamming the shifter into drive, she took off, dust spewing from the tires as she bumped over the rutted road through the trees.

Her heartbeat thudded like a drum inside her chest, blood rushing in her ears as she tried to collect her scattered thoughts. She needed to get to a phone as quickly as possible. She had to reach Detective Tillet and give him her location before Travis managed to flee the scene. He wouldn't get far on foot, but it wouldn't be long before Dillon returned and they had a vehicle at their disposal.

Keeping the accelerator depressed as far to the floorboard as she dared on the dirt road, Haley concentrated on reaching the gravel road that led out of the woods. Every bone in her body rattled as her car hurtled forward. The minute she felt gravel beneath her tires, she floored the engine, oblivious to the rock chips peppering the fenders like gunfire. Beyond the woods, flat agricultural fields stretched out in every direction, nothing but a couple of ramshackle barns in sight. She estimated she couldn't be more than a few miles at most from the main road into town. Heartened by her escape, she clutched the steering wheel tighter and increased her speed again.

She took the next bend in the road too fast, spinning on the gravel and almost losing control entirely. She slowed her speed a tad, fearing she would crash, and her brazen escape attempt would all have been for nothing. Up ahead, another vehicle appeared on the horizon. A tiny speck traveling in her direction. Her chest tightened. Should she flag the driver down for help or keep going to the nearest house? As the car drew closer, she caught a glimpse of the face through the windscreen, belatedly recognizing the sedan Dillon had driven away in. She gritted her teeth. He'd recognized her too and was making a beeline for her, flashing his lights.

Terror gripped her when she realized his intention was probably to run her off the road. Gripping the wheel, she held her course for as long as possible and then, at the last second, swerved off the gravel into the neighboring field, narrowly avoiding colliding with the sedan. Immediately, she steered her car back onto the road and accelerated before Dillon had a chance to turn around.

Glancing in the rear-view mirror, she caught sight of a cloud of dust like a mini tornado whipping up behind her as

Dillon spun his vehicle around. Terrified she wouldn't make it to the main road before he caught up with her, Haley floored the engine again until she was dancing on the verge of losing control. Despite her valiant attempt to outrun him, she could hear the roar of his engine gaining on her. Seconds later, there was a sickening crunch of metal as he rammed into her bumper. Only the seat belt held her in place as her body was flung forward and then backward. Fighting for control, she increased her speed again, this time focused on putting as much distance as possible between her and Dillon rather than on keeping control of the vehicle. If she gave him the chance to immobilize her car, her only protection would be gone, and he'd waste no time in finishing her off.

To her horror, he began to gain on her even more rapidly, slamming into her again with more force than before. She screamed as her car spun around in the gravel, tires squealing. When she looked through the windshield, she was facing back the way she'd come.

Dillon had already climbed out of his car and was beating a path toward her, waving his arms frantically. For a brief moment, Haley froze, her brain unable to function or direct her. He seized the advantage, swiftly descending on her vehicle. Haley clenched her jaw, her resolve hardening. She wasn't about to give up. She wouldn't cower and die without a fight.

Forcing the shifter into reverse, she tore back down the gravel road away from him. She could feel the fender scraping on the wheel where Dillon had rammed his vehicle into it, but she closed her mind to the unnatural sound and focused her thoughts solely on making her escape. Dillon turned and ran back to his car. He would be after her in a matter of seconds. She needed to turn her car around to get to the main road, but that would cost her precious time. She wouldn't be able to outdrive him anyway. He'd already proved his car was faster than hers. Her only hope was to take him by surprise and beat him at his own game.

Slamming on the brakes she shifted into drive and depressed the accelerator. Engine screaming, she motored straight toward Dillon, eyes firmly fixed on her goal.

Doggedly holding her course, she stared down the approaching sedan. Something faltered in Dillon's expression, his eyes widening when he realized she wasn't trying to evade him—this time she was heading straight for him. For a second, he lost momentum as he tried to change direction and swerve out of her path. Haley floored the accelerator, sideswiping his car. Her head jerked violently at the impact, wrenching her neck, but she clung to the wheel with sweating fingers, somehow managing to hold her course. When she glanced in the rearview mirror again, she saw Dillon's car flip and career into the adjacent field.

Alternate waves of relief and nausea coursed through her. She wheeled around and accelerated past the wreck, sobbing as she drove, desperately trying to wipe the blinding tears from her eyes with the back of her sleeve so she could see the road ahead. At long last, a swathe of asphalt loomed in front of her. She peeled out onto the main road and raced toward the small cluster of businesses and houses that comprised the town a couple of miles ahead.

Somehow, she'd made it out alive, but she needed to get help. Despite everything Dillon had done, she wasn't going to leave him to suffer and die on the side of the road. Or Travis either—if he hadn't already succumbed to the brutal blow she'd inflicted on him.

30

*H*aley clutched the paper cup of coffee between her fingers and sipped the hot liquid gratefully as Detective Tillet took her statement the following day. At her feet lay Katniss who'd refused to leave her side since their euphoric reunion. Natalie was waiting in the reception area, ready to drive her home afterward, not willing to take no for an answer, as always.

"What else are friends for?" she'd insisted. "You're exhausted and in shock. Trust me, you'll need a chauffeur and a shoulder to cry on after Detective Tillet's done with you."

Local police had apprehended Travis and Dillon Ramsey without incident. Travis had been found inside the trailer, disoriented, and nursing a head wound and a blinding headache. Things had deteriorated once he'd been taken to the hospital, and he'd been put on suicide watch after threatening to kill himself. Dillon had been extricated from his vehicle, unconscious but remarkably without any serious injuries other than a broken arm.

"I won't be charged with assault, will I?" Haley asked.

"No, you were the victim. You did what you had to do to get away," Detective Tillet reassured her. "They'll be discharged from the hospital into police custody as soon as they've recovered sufficiently. At that point, they'll be formally charged."

"With kidnapping?"

"And intent to murder. As co-conspirators, they'll both be locked up for a long time. We did a thorough search of the trailer and Dillon's vehicle and found all the items they bought: shovels, tarp, duct tape, plastic sheeting." Detective Tillet hesitated. "And the noose on the ladder. We were also able to retrieve messages from burner phones in their possession detailing their plan to kill you and bury your body in the woods nearby."

A tremor crossed Haley's shoulders.

"We'll still need your testimony to bring them to justice," Detective Tillet said.

Haley averted her gaze. She wasn't sure how she felt about going to court and seeing her husband on the stand. It was still incomprehensible to her that he had married her with the sole intention of terrorizing her and ultimately killing her.

"My officers can't stop talking about how you singlehand-edly escaped from that trailer and left them both hospital-ized," Detective Tillet said good-humoredly. "I guess your self-defense training paid off in the end."

Haley grimaced. "It's called desperation. I got lucky. Things could have turned out very differently."

"Let's start at the beginning," Detective Tillet said, resting one ankle over his knee. "When did you first meet Dillon Ramsey?"

Haley sipped her coffee, mustering up the courage it would take to finally admit to what she'd covered up for so long. Quashing her misgivings, she began to fill Detective

Tillet in on the connection between the brothers and what she had done back in high school. She explained how Travis had dated one of her quad sisters and found out who'd been behind the prank that had gone so terribly wrong—the dark secret she'd spent her whole life running from. As she feared, telling the story brought up a lot of unresolved pain, and she broke down more than once, forced to take multiple breaks before she finally stumbled through it.

When she finished, she let out a ragged breath, ready to face the consequences of her actions. "Are you ... going to reopen the investigation?"

Detective Tillet rubbed his jaw thoughtfully. "You didn't commit a crime, Haley. Even back then, you and your friends couldn't have been prosecuted for Emma's death. Your actions, regrettable as they were, wouldn't have been enough to warrant an arrest. I'm not going to reopen the investigation into Emma Murray's suicide, but you need to be prepared to deal with the fallout once the press connect the dots between the two stories. This is the kind of stuff they eat up."

Haley swallowed hard. "Yeah, I'm sure I'll lose my job over this, but I deserve whatever they throw at me. I should have owned up to what I did back then. If I'd paid the price at the time, it would never have come to this." She ran a hand through her hair in an agitated fashion. "I thought I was protecting myself by covering it up all these years, but the cost was so much greater in the end. Not just to me, but to Emma's parents. They've lost everything now."

Detective Tillet squared his jaw. "You're not responsible for what Travis and Dillon did. They allowed their bitterness to cloud their judgement."

A knock on the door interrupted them, and a young female officer stuck her head around the door. She raised a brow at Detective Tillet. "Can I have a word, sir?"

He threw Haley an apologetic look. "Hold that thought. I'll be right back."

She nodded, and slumped back in her chair. Her quad sisters would be both relieved and shocked to learn that her stalker—her husband—had been apprehended. No doubt the press would harangue them too once the details came out, but it was a small price to pay for what they'd all done.

When Detective Tillet reappeared a few minutes later, he didn't immediately resume where they'd left off. Instead, he drummed his fingers on the desk, a strained expression on his face. "There's someone here who wants to speak to you. To be honest, I'm not sure how you're going to feel about it."

Haley frowned, her heartbeat picking up pace. It couldn't be Dillon—Detective Tillet said he'd be taken into custody as soon as the hospital released him. Her parents were flying in from Florida, but their flight didn't get here until late afternoon. And Natalie was already at the station waiting to drive her home. "Who is it?" she asked tentatively.

"It's Dillon's mother."

Haley's eyebrows shot up. "Caroline Murray?" An icy fear gripped her at the thought of seeing Emma's mother again. There could only be one reason why she'd come—to look in the face of the woman who had driven her daughter to take her own life and tell her how much she hated her.

"Do I have to see her?" Haley asked, a plaintive note creeping into her voice.

Detective Tillet shrugged. "Your call. But this might be your chance to put things right. You've been telling me about the guilt you've been dragging around like a ball and chain all these years."

Haley raked her fingernails over her cheeks distractedly. "I'm sure she despises me now that she knows the truth. She'd probably like to finish what her sons started, and I wouldn't blame her."

Detective Tillet hefted his brows and folded his arms across his chest. "She's hardly going to attack you here. Besides, she's old and frail. Your newly-acquired self-defense moves could take her out in a heartbeat."

Haley gave a wry grin. "I know I'm being a coward trying to wriggle my way out of this meeting." She took a deep breath and then slowly let the air leak back out of her lungs. Over the years, she'd imagined this day a thousand times, in a thousand different ways, but none of them had played out like this with her coming face-to-face with Emma's mother. Nevertheless, Detective Tillet was right. For what it was worth, this was her chance to extend a heartfelt apology for her role in what had happened.

"Okay, I'll talk to her. Will you stay in the room with us?"

"Sure, if that's what you want," Detective Tillet replied, getting to his feet. "I'll fetch her."

After he'd left the room, Haley laid her head down on the desk, her cheek pressed against the cool steel of the table, her thoughts drifting back to her sophomore year, and the day she'd pinned Emma's most secret dreams to the notice board outside Mr. Davidson's classroom. A single act that had ruined her teacher's life as well—destroyed his reputation and career. Everything about that fateful day would be forever imprinted on her mind. She could still smell the interior of Lachlan's new Prius and the cheap perfume Emma had sprayed on the pages of her diary. Sickening odors that swirled together in a concentrate that made her stomach roil. Smells that could transport her back to her fifteen-year-old self in half a heartbeat.

She startled at an abrupt knock, quickly straightening up in her chair. The door opened and Detective Tillet escorted Caroline Murray inside. Her tired eyes locked with Haley's, her expression unreadable as she shuffled across to the table and sat down heavily in a chair opposite her.

Haley shifted uncomfortably in her seat, waiting for Detective Tillet to say something to initiate the conversation, but he leaned against the wall at the back of the room, signaling that he was only there as a spectator—at best to referee any potential situations that might arise.

Caroline's puckered lips opened and closed a couple of times before the words began to flow, "I'm so terribly sorry for what my sons did to you, dear. I can't even begin to imagine how terrified you must have been tied up in that trailer not knowing what was going to happen next."

Salty tears trickled down Haley's cheeks as the horror of her ordeal came rushing back. She hung her head and shook it slowly. "I'm the one who should be apologizing to you. It was me who tore the page out of Emma's diary and pinned it to the notice board. I can never forgive myself for what I did."

Caroline's gnarled hand reached out across the table and squeezed her arm gently. "I know, dear, that's why I wanted to speak with you. It's time to let the past go and forgive yourself. Detective Tillet told me you've been blaming yourself for my daughter's death all these years, but the truth is, Emma wanted to kill herself long before you found her diary. She was a wonderful girl, and gifted in many ways, but she was fragile—she struggled with depression and suicidal thoughts. It wasn't the first time she'd tried to kill herself. She'd been in and out of counseling for years."

Haley stared at Caroline in shock, trying to absorb her words. If she was understanding this right, Emma's mother wasn't condemning her for what she'd done at all. Quite the opposite—she was absolving her of any blame in Emma's death. A lone tear slid down her cheek at the woman's kindness in the face of her own pain.

"What I did was still a despicable thing, I'm deeply ashamed of it. I was a cowardly bully," Haley said. "The only thing I can say in my defense is that I'm not that person anymore. Believe me, I've done everything in my power since to make amends."

Caroline smiled warmly, her paper-thin skin stretched across her jaw. "Yes, I know you have. Detective Tillet told me all about your work with Big Brothers Big Sisters. I'm proud of you, dear. You took the wrong you did and turned it into something beautiful. Unfortunately, my boys chose to do the opposite. They let the pain of their sister's suicide fester inside them until they turned into the very monsters they'd built you up in their minds to be."

"How can you be so forgiving of me?" Haley asked.

Caroline tweaked a sad smile. "I first had to learn to forgive myself for not being a better mother, for not noticing the signs that day, for not knowing about Emma's infatuation with a teacher. In retrospect, there were so many things I could blame myself for. But, at the end of the day, I had to accept that the choice she made was her own. There's always a right way and a wrong way to deal with our problems. Sadly, Emma chose the wrong way, and she hurt a lot of other people in the process, including all the people who loved her most."

Haley sucked on her lip, struggling to hold back the deluge of tears threatening to spill.

"So, you see," Caroline continued, "it wasn't hard to forgive you. You were a fifteen-year-old child, trying to find your way, just like my Emma. I don't hold what you did against you. Living with bitterness is a kind of death in itself. We all make mistakes and do stupid things we regret, and I've learned that people can change, for better or for worse."

"Thank you," Haley managed to squeeze out between sobs.

Caroline patted Haley's hands between her own. "I want you to promise me that you'll put this behind you now and move forward with your life—for Emma's sake. Live the life she chose to give up on and live it to the fullest."

Haley blinked back her tears and nodded. "What about your husband? Can he ever forgive me?"

Caroline smiled. "Ronnie never held anything against you to begin with. He always said that whoever had posted that diary page would be haunted for the rest of their lives by what they'd done, and he only prayed they could forgive themselves."

"He sounds like a wonderful man," Haley said, gulping back another sob.

"He is indeed—and a wonderful husband." Caroline's eyes twinkled. "Maybe you'll come back and visit us again some time. He'd enjoy meeting you.

Haley gave a tight smile but said nothing. She appreciated Caroline reaching out to her, but she wasn't sure that was a promise she could keep. For now, at least, she needed to cut all ties to Dillon, and that meant everything and everyone associated with him as well.

Both brothers would serve long prison terms for kidnapping and conspiracy to murder. At last, she was free of her stalkers and their campaign of terror, but, more importantly, she was free of the ghosts of her past that had shadowed her through the years and held her hostage to a burden of guilt that had never been hers to bear. Emma Murray was a broken soul long before they crossed paths. Haley only wished she'd been strong enough to reach out a helping hand to her instead of contributing to her pain.

Going forward, she was determined to become the type of friend she should have been years ago—the type of friend she had waiting for her in Natalie. She would start by baking Lance a big plate of cookies. She owed him big time for his many acts of kindness, and for watching out for her. After that, she would make a concerted effort to try and persuade

Edith to move out of the house she shared with her loath-
some brother, and begin life afresh. Together, they could find
somewhere safe for her to live. Finally, she would reach out
to her quad sisters and put them out of their misery. At last,
they were all free of the dark cloud that had hung over them
for all these years.

And maybe one day, when she'd managed to put all this
behind her, she might even find love again. Until then, she
had the best companion a woman could ask for. She leaned
down and ruffled Katniss's ears. "Don't worry, girl, we're a
package deal from now on. If I ever fall in love again, it will
only be with a man who loves you first."

31

*S*hortly after ten the following morning, Haley's phone began to vibrate. She set down her coffee mug on the kitchen counter and unplugged her phone from the wall outlet, frowning when Detective Tillet's number came up on the screen.

"Dillon's awake and lucid," he said when she took his call. "The officer outside his room notified me a few minutes ago. I know this won't be easy for you. I didn't want you hearing it from anyone else first."

Haley swallowed back the bile rising up her throat. Much as she hated to admit it, part of her had hoped her husband would succumb to his injuries and spare her the agony of a trial where she'd be forced to testify against him. She couldn't deny she still had feelings for him, despite what he'd done. It was hard to hate the man you'd loved enough to marry without some level of wavering between regret and rage. "Thank you for letting me know," she managed, her throat like sandpaper.

Detective Tillet coughed discreetly. "I also wanted to inform you that there's been a development."

Haley's thoughts raced in myriad directions. What now? Had Travis managed to kill himself like he'd threatened to do? Had her husband suffered a traumatic brain injury and forgotten what he'd done now that he was awake? That would be awfully convenient. She almost didn't want to know what was coming next. "What kind of ... development?"

"I think you'll be surprised to hear that your husband told us a very different story to yours."

Haley gasped. "What are you talking about? Don't tell me he tried to deny what happened in the trailer—because if—"

"No, nothing like that," Detective Tillet interrupted. "In fact, he confirmed everything you told us, but he swears he was trying to stop Travis. He was only playing along with him so he could go into town and get help. He said he made up some excuse about forgetting to pick up the supplies so he could alert the authorities."

"What?" Haley sank back on her couch, her thoughts flitting back and forth like shooting stars inside her brain. "That doesn't make any sense. Why didn't he stop Travis before he abducted me."

"He claims he didn't know Travis was planning to abduct you that day. And when he arrived at the trailer, Travis was armed. He had no choice but to pretend to go along with him in order to buy some time."

"Of course he's going to say that," Haley responded, exasperated. "He's trying to put all the blame on Travis now that he's been caught so that—"

"Actually," Detective Tillet cut in. "His iPhone records—not the burner phone—show that he made a call to the police right before you did, as soon as he got close enough to town to pick up service. He warned the cops that Travis was armed. Then he headed back to check on you. That's when he encountered you on the road. He says he flashed his lights to try and get you to stop. When you didn't, he was afraid Travis had abducted you and was forcing you to drive at gunpoint. That's why he tried to stop you by ramming your car. The officers who responded to the scene of the accident were already responding to his call when yours came in."

Haley fell silent grappling with the enormity of what she was hearing. If she was understanding Detective Tillet's drift, Dillon was saying he hadn't been in cahoots with his brother after all. He'd been trying to help her. Could it be true? Her heart tripped with a sudden surge of renewed hope. Was it possible he hadn't wanted to kill her, that, in fact, he'd laid everything on the line in an attempt to save her?

"We're still investigating all this, of course," Detective Tillet continued. "But, so far, your husband's story is checking out. He sent multiple text messages over the past few weeks to his brother telling him to back off and leave you both alone. Naturally, he'll still face charges for obstruction and concealing evidence."

"I don't know what to say," Haley whispered. "My emotions are all over the place. Up until a few days ago, I believed my husband loved me. Then I found out he was trying to kill me. Now, you're telling me he was only pretending to help his brother, in a bid to save me."

Detective Tillet grunted. "It's a crazy situation, but that's how it appears. We're still sifting through all the evidence to make sure his story checks out, but I can tell you that, so far, Travis has confirmed everything your husband told us." He paused and then added softly. "He's been asking for you. Do you want to talk to him? We'd be very interested in hearing how he explains it all to you."

"I ... I'm not sure ... I mean, I suppose so."

"You'll be perfectly safe," Detective Tillet assured her. "There's an officer stationed outside his room. We're not taking any chances until we have clarity on the situation and he's been cleared of all kidnapping and attempted murder charges."

Haley chewed on her lip. "What about Travis?"

"He's been granted bail, but he'll be fitted with a tracking device as one of his conditions of bail so you don't have to worry about him trying to finish what he started."

Haley scrunched her eyes shut, scarcely able to grasp this sudden turn of events. "I guess I'll head to the hospital and see what my husband has to say for himself."

"Call me after you've talked to him."

Haley hung up and drove to the hospital in a daze, trying to gather her thoughts into some semblance of order. Had Dillon been attempting to protect her by pretending to go along with Travis's insidious plan? Her heart ached for the husband she'd loved and thought she'd lost. Was it possible he'd truly loved her all along?

She parked in the hospital parking structure and stuffed her ticket into her purse with a gnawing sense of trepidation. She was equal parts desperate to see her husband, yet filled with dread at the thought of coming face to face with him again. She wasn't sure how she would feel when she walked into his room and saw firsthand what she'd done to him by running him off the road. She'd never intentionally harmed another human being before—let alone hurt someone she cared about. And now it seemed he was innocent of any part in the twisted plot his brother had cooked up—that he'd actually come to the trailer to save her. But, how could she have known that? It had been a terrifying ordeal, and if Dillon truly loved her, he wouldn't hold it against her—he would understand exactly why she'd had to do what she'd done to save herself.

Haley checked in with reception and made her way up to the second floor to her husband's room. She nodded to the officer on duty outside and volunteered her ID before pushing open the door. Inside, the room smelled of antiseptic and stale chemical cleaning odors. Her eyes fastened on Dillon lying on the bed, eyes closed, his left arm in a cast, his face bruised and swollen. Haley recoiled at the sight, momentarily taken aback at the damage she'd inflicted. She flinched when his eyes suddenly fluttered open. They traveled, unfocused, around the room before they alighted on her loitering by the door. "Sweetheart," he rasped. "You're safe."

Haley pressed her lips tightly together to keep the hot tears that immediately welled up from spilling down her cheeks. There was no denying the emotion in his voice. It was the old Jake, her beloved husband calling her sweetheart. Travis had scoffed at that term of endearment, sowing doubt and discord in her mind, but it felt right when Jake whispered it, like it always had. "Yes, I'm safe," she whispered back. "I'm ... so sorry, babe ... I thought ..."

Dillon closed his eyes briefly. "Don't say anything more, you have absolutely nothing to apologize for. I should have told you everything from the beginning." He gestured at the chair next to his bed. "Sit down. I owe you a proper explanation."

Haley's shoulders heaved up and down. They both owed each other the truth at this point. "I take it you know what I did to Emma?"

Dillon gave a tentative nod, wincing as if even the smallest exertion pained him. "I wanted revenge at first, just like Travis, but after a while I came to see things from my mother's point of view. You were only a kid yourself, you didn't know Emma's history, you weren't to blame for what she did. She would have found another excuse to do it sooner or later." He brushed a hand across his jaw, his voice breaking. "Travis, on the other hand, refused to relent. On his twenty-first birthday, he even stuck a gun in his mouth and threatened to kill himself if I didn't help him hunt down Emma's killer."

Haley pressed a hand to her mouth. She wanted to reach out and comfort her husband, but another part of her wanted to wait until she'd heard the rest of his story.

"I agreed, only to placate him. I was afraid he'd do something stupid if I didn't pretend I was on board. I never thought we'd actually find out anything," Dillon continued. "My mother and I tried to get Travis help, many times over the years, but he wouldn't go to counseling. When he finally tracked you down, I asked you out on a date as a way to get close to you. The truth is, I was trying to figure out a way to protect you, to warn you, and then ... " He let out a sigh and fixed his gaze on Haley. "Then I fell for you."

Tears trailed down her cheeks. She leaned forward and rested her head on her husband's chest, sobbing silently for several minutes as he ran his fingers tenderly through her hair. "I'm so sorry, Hales. I should never have put you at risk. It was the dumbest thing I've ever done. I thought I could handle the situation and talk sense into Travis. I was trying to spare him from going to prison." He shook his head sadly. "You have to understand where I was coming from, Mom's lost so much already. In retrospect, I should have went straight to the police."

"You knew it was him, all the time?" Haley asked.

"Yes, but I never once thought he would take it to the next level and try to kill you. I managed to talk him into backing off for a while after we got married. But when he attacked me that night, I knew he was too dangerous to be trusted. I was working on having him committed. You have to believe me, Hales, I swear, if I'd thought for even one minute—"

She pressed a finger to his lips. "Shh! Don't say another word. I believe you. Detective Tillet told me about your phone records. I know you were only trying to help me."

Dillon squeezed his eyes shut and brushed the back of his hand across his face. "Travis won't be able to hurt us any more. He won't be getting out of prison for a very long time."

"I know," Haley said softly. "We can start over, put all this behind us." She leaned over and kissed her husband gently on the forehead. "You need to rest now." She picked up her purse from the floor and got to her feet. "I'll be back in the morning with some clothes and toiletries."

"Thank you, sweetheart." Dillon smiled weakly and then sank back in his pillows watching as Haley exited the room with a final wave.

Back in her car, she gripped the steering wheel tightly, her eyes brimming with tears. She'd almost killed the man she loved, and it had all been a horrible misunderstanding. He'd sacrificed everything to try and protect her. She didn't blame him in the least for trying to protect Travis too. He'd been trying to salvage what was left of his broken family— she could hardly fault him for that. In fact, she loved him all the more for it. She started up the engine and dialed Detective Tillet.

DILLON FISHED out his phone and hit the speed dial for his brother's phone. It rang three times before Travis picked up. "I was beginning to think you weren't going to pull through, bro. Last I heard she left you in a coma."

Dillon grunted. "I'm tougher than you give me credit for. Besides, I was milking my injuries."

"Evidently. What's the word?"

"Our backup plan with the phones worked. The cops think I'm the good guy."

"And *sweetheart*?"

"She bought it too," Dillon replied. "I'm being discharged in the morning."

"Great, I picked up the passports. You know where to find yours. I'll be waiting."

"Order me a margarita. I'll be there as soon as I finish what we started."

———

(FOR ALL MY GENTLE READERS who prefer a happy ending with justice served, I have included a BONUS CHAPTER 32 just for you!)

———

BONUS CHAPTER ALTERNATE ENDING

*H*aley sat stunned in her plastic seat at the police station as Detective Tillet replayed the recorded conversation between Dillon and Travis back to her. The words seemed to reverberate around the room.

"And sweetheart?"

"She bought it too."

"Order me a margarita. I'll be there as soon as I finish what we started."

Her thoughts were catapulting her to a place she didn't want to go. *No! No! No!* How could Dillon have betrayed her like this? More important, how had she allowed herself to be duped by him twice over? Was she really that desperate to be loved that she'd allowed herself to buy into his treacherous fantasy?

Her shoulders shook as she tried to come to terms with what she had just been forced to listen to. There was no coming back from it. Dillon had conspired with Travis to kill her.

"I had my suspicions all along," Detective Tillet said, his tone apologetic. "Which is why I had their phones tapped. It was all just too convenient. I'm sorry, Haley. I know this isn't what you wanted to hear. But I couldn't warn you ahead of time. I had to pretend I'd bought their whole story. Otherwise, Dillon would have known right away something was amiss when you talked to him. He's extremely adept at reading people."

Haley stared at the floor as she rubbed her brow with her fingertips. "I feel so stupid. How could I not have seen through him?"

"For what it's worth, you had the same distorted view of him that everyone else did. He cultivated an empathetic image, and he was extremely effective at it."

"In retrospect, I realize my biggest mistake was rushing into the relationship," Haley said. "I quashed any doubts I had out of fear of being alone. It was terrifying knowing someone was stalking me. I thought I would be safer with Jake—I mean, Dillon—by my side. I convinced myself I loved him before I even knew him properly. Turns out I didn't even know his real name."

"In your defense, he was very persuasive—a master manipulator," Detective Tillet responded. "I've met psychopaths like him before. They're not all the crazy-eyed Jack-the-Ripper maniacs Hollywood makes them out to be. They're often charming and well-liked. They portray themselves as model citizens, mimicking all the right behavior while they dupe people with their lies."

Haley bit her lip. "Dillon did a good job of that. I actually thought he cared for me. He showed me such empathy at times."

Detective Tillet cleared his throat. "I'm sorry it turned out to be a farce. He learned everything he could about you before he contrived a way to meet you. He probably made you feel like you were soulmates after your first conversation."

Haley nodded thoughtfully. "You're right. He had a sob story about his parents dying in an accident. That endeared me to him from the outset. He seemed so broken over it."

Detective Tillet grunted. "He knew how to milk empathy, like every good psychopath does."

Haley let out a long, shuddering sigh. "What will happen to him now?"

"That's up to the court to decide. Mental illness runs in his family, so I'm sure that will be used as a defense. Either way, he'll be locked up somewhere for a long time to come."

Haley tilted a brow upward. "And Travis?"

"His bail was revoked. He's already been apprehended. Don't worry, you're perfectly safe now."

Haley reached for her purse. "I can't thank you enough for everything you've done—especially for believing me."

Detective Tillet's expression softened as he stretched out a hand. "It's time you started believing in yourself again. Do we have a deal?"

Haley grinned, blinking back tears as she shook his hand. "Absolutely. I'm ready to make peace with my past. It's in the rearview mirror now."

She exited Detective Tillet's office and made her way out of the police station into the crisp morning air, smiling spontaneously at a couple exchanging a quick kiss as they strolled by, arm-in-arm, with a Golden Retriever puppy on a leash.

She would learn to trust like that again one day too, but first she had to learn to trust herself. No doubt, she would flounder at times along the way. But, she would choose to forgive her mistakes. No one else could make her whole. More important, no one else could take her down when the courage to spread her wings and fly again came from within.

Ready for another gripping read? Check out my heart-stopping thriller **Her Last Steps**

Trust no one when your daughter goes missing.

On a frigid winter morning near her cabin, Ava Galbraith's four-year-old daughter vanishes without a trace in the snow. Local sheriff, Mallory Anderson, focuses his initial investigation on Ava and her estranged husband, Gordon, embroiled in a bitter custody battle. But when Ava receives a ransom demand for half-a-million dollars, the race to find four-year-old Melanie takes on a more ominous tone. With the FBI on board, disturbing secrets begin to emerge connecting both Ava and her husband to a murky past. A remote cabin in the woods may hold some desperately needed answers, but time is ticking down to complete the ransom drop-off and save Melanie from the one person who wants her dead.

Who is the real mastermind behind the abduction?

- Fasten your seatbelt for a tense domestic thriller with a heart-pounding pace! -

Do you enjoy reading across genres? I also write young adult science fiction and fantasy thrillers. You can find out more about those titles on my website.

www.normahinkens.com

A QUICK FAVOR...

Dear Reader,

I hope you enjoyed reading *The Lies She Told* as much as I enjoyed writing it. Thank you for taking the time to check out my books and I would appreciate it from the bottom of my heart if you would leave a review, long or short, here on Amazon as it makes a HUGE difference in helping new readers find the series. Thank you!

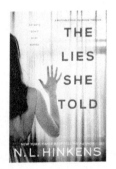

To be the first to hear about my upcoming book releases, sales, and fun giveaways, sign up for my Newsletter here. You can find me on the web at www.normahinkens.com and follow me on Twitter, Instagram and Facebook. Feel free to email me at norma@normahinkens.com with any feedback or comments. I LOVE hearing from readers. YOU are the reason I keep going through the tough times.

All my best,
Norma

HER LAST STEPS

Ready for another suspense-filled read? Check out my heart-stopping thriller *Her Last Steps* on Amazon!

Trust no one when your daughter goes missing.
On a frigid winter morning near her cabin, Ava Galbraith's four-year-old daughter vanishes without a trace in the snow. Local sheriff, Mallory Anderson, focuses his initial investigation on Ava and her estranged husband, Gordon, embroiled in a bitter custody battle. But when Ava receives a

ransom demand for half-a-million dollars, the race to find four-year-old Melanie takes on a more ominous tone. With the FBI on board, disturbing secrets begin to emerge connecting both Ava and her husband to a murky past. A remote cabin in the woods may hold some desperately needed answers, but time is ticking down to complete the ransom drop-off and save Melanie from the one person who wants her dead.

Who is the real mastermind behind the abduction?
- Fasten your seatbelt for a tense domestic thriller with a heart-pounding pace! -

---

Do you enjoy reading across genres? I also write young adult science fiction and fantasy thrillers. You can find out more about those titles at **www.normahinkens.com.**

A QUICK FAVOR

Dear Reader,

I hope you enjoyed reading *The Lies She Told* as much as I enjoyed writing it. Thank you for taking the time to check out my books and I would appreciate it from the bottom of my heart if you would leave a review, long or short, on Amazon as it makes a HUGE difference in helping new readers find the series. Thank you!

To be the first to hear about my upcoming book releases, sales, and fun giveaways, sign up for my newsletter at **www.normahinkens.com** and follow me on Twitter, Instagram and Facebook. Feel free to email me at norma@normahinkens.com with any feedback or comments. I LOVE hearing from readers. YOU are the reason I keep going through the tough times.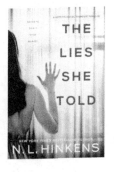

All my best,

Norma

BIOGRAPHY

NYT and USA Today bestselling author Norma Hinkens writes twisty psychological suspense thrillers, as well as fast-paced science fiction and fantasy about spunky heroines and epic adventures in dangerous worlds. She's also a travel junkie, legend lover, and idea wrangler, in no particular order. She grew up in Ireland, land of make-believe and the original little green man.

Find out more about her books on her website.
www.normahinkens.com

Follow her on Facebook for funnies, giveaways, cool stuff & more!

BOOKS BY NORMA HINKENS

I also write young adult science fiction and fantasy thrillers under Norma Hinkens.

www.normahinkens.com/books

THE UNDERGROUNDERS SERIES - POST-APOCALYPTIC
Immurement
Embattlement
Judgement

THE EXPULSION PROJECT - SCIENCE FICTION
Girl of Fire
Girl of Stone
Girl of Blood

THE KEEPERS CHRONICLES - EPIC FANTASY
Opal of Light
Onyx of Darkness
Opus of Doom

FOLLOW NORMA:

Sign up for her newsletter:

https://books.normahinkens.com/VIPReaderClub

Website:

https://normahinkens.com/

Facebook:

https://www.facebook.com/NormaHinkensAuthor/

Twitter

https://twitter.com/NormaHinkens

Instagram

https://www.instagram.com/normahinkensauthor/

Pinterest:

https://www.pinterest.com/normahinkens/

Made in the USA
Coppell, TX
15 May 2021